# Springtime in Hades

K. Lynn Bay

Flying Tiger Press

flyingtigerpress.com

Cover art by Renee McHugh
www.remdesigns.com

To my mom, who was always a romantic at heart.

# Acknowlegements

Where do I start? Closest to home, I guess. Thanks to my husband, Bob, who always reads my stories even though they aren't his thing, gives me plenty of space to write them and good, common sense to go on with. To fellow writers Laura Carlson and LaVonne Jordan for their keen eyes and perceptive comments. We've gone so far and grown so much together. And to my dad, Don Bay, my first reader and excellent proofreader. You guys, I couldn't do it without you.

# I

I guess most girls dream of riding off into the sunset with their handsome prince. Well, maybe not most. Some are proper Amazons who consider men a necessary evil at best and a flat-out nuisance at worst. And probably a few fantasize about carrying the *guy* off.

Me, I'll admit it. I'm old-fashioned. I always secretly liked the idea of being swept off my feet. The problem is, being whisked away by a tall, dark stranger is a lot more attractive in theory than in fact. My mom, Demetra, says it was my uncle Zeusse who caused the whole mess. But after all the stuff she did, of course someone else has to be the villain. I'm more philosophical. If I had to put the blame anywhere, it'd be on my magic.

My name is Persephonie—Perry, for short. I'm an earth sorceress, although for a while we thought I might not be. A sorceress, that is. And that's where the trouble started.

You see, most sorcerers' powers come to them around the age of fourteen or fifteen. With me, sixteen passed and I still didn't show any sorcerous tendencies. Seventeen. By eighteen, I'd pretty much given up hope. (So had my mom, though she'd never admit it.) When my powers finally put in their appearance about a week before my nineteenth birthday, we were ready to throw a party and invite the whole neighborhood, even if regular people— non-sorcerers, I mean—do tend to get a mite exercised when confronted with real, live magic.

Then came the bad news. My powers were a little, shall we say, extreme. Wherever I went—yowsa!— things *grew*. Actually, "grew" is an understatement. More like exploded, doing what life does but with lustful abandon. The kind of magic Mom does, only without the control and subtlety.

About three months after my big questionable pre-birthday gift, I came home to find Uncle Zeusse sitting at the kitchen table drinking a beer. *Oh, yay*, I thought. As far as I'm concerned, the longer between Uncle Zeusse's visits, the better I like it.

Mom was standing at the sink doing something with herbs—I could smell them, a scent somewhere between lemon and mint.

Zeusse looks like a biker who works out: wavy hair to his shoulders, a big curly reddish beard and muscles that strain just about any shirt he puts on. He does not have a biker paunch. His fingers are stained yellow from smoking, but Mom wouldn't (and won't) let him smoke in her house, even if it was only a little three-room stucco thing with ancient linoleum floors and small, wavy-glassed windows like it was then.

Zeusse eyed me that way he has that says he's about to say something really obnoxious. I was wearing jeans and a tank top. Maybe the jeans are too tight, I think. Or maybe the tank top is a little, um, small for my figure. Let's put it this way: it didn't quite reach the waistband of my jeans, and my bra didn't quite show. Sure enough, here came the obnoxious comment, but it wasn't what I expected. He said, "Perry, you need a husband."

I blinked. "What?"

He drummed his fingers on his beer can: *pap-pap-pap-pap*. "I'm talking about your powers."

Oh. Great. For three months, Mom and I talked about nothing but. Like how I'd cross a field of thumb-high corn and you could tell exactly where I'd walked, because there'd be this perfect path of rich green taller than me bursting with plump ears. Or the way trees would suddenly burst into leaf and fruit would puff up like popcorn.

All that was awkward enough, but it got worse when people I'd pass on the street would fall into clinches behind me as if some were wearing steel clothes and others were covered with super-powerful magnets.

Now Zeusse wanted to weigh in.

Mom had her back to me, but I could tell she was pissed—it was like this green gas rising from her head.

She turned and gave Zeusse a look that can blight crops. "She does *not* need a husband. She simply needs time to explore her abilities."

I looked over my shoulder. Through the screen door, I saw two dogs humping in the gravel drive of our little cul-de-sac off the main road. The smell of jasmine had followed me into the house, so I knew the star jasmine bushes by the front door had again overgrown the walk in my wake. No doubt our little patch of lawn was knee-high, too.

"Mom isn't married, and she doesn't have any trouble with her powers." I said it very innocently.

People generally think I'm as green as they come. I can get away with all kinds of impertinence.

"No," he said. "She isn't a virgin, either."

I'd walked right into that one, but that was ruder than usual. So rude, in fact, my brain was still cranking away at a sufficiently outraged response when Mom slapped the herbs into the sink. With a tang of mint, green dust puffed into the air.

"Zeusse," she said sharply. "My daughter will make her own choices and tame her power in her own way. I will not have you inflicting your Neanderthal views on her."

"You will if you don't want the duds following a path of rampant greenery straight to the doorstep of two sorceresses," he shot back.

"Duds" is what some sorcerers call regular people. I used the term once and Mom took my power of speech for a whole day. At the moment, however, I was occupied with going hot from the neckline of my tank top to my hairline.

"Just because you have to do it with somebody to make *your* magic work doesn't mean everybody else does." I tried to sound like my usual sweet self, but it came out sounding like honey laced with strychnine.

"And since I don't tell you how to handle your magic, I'd appreciate it if you don't tell me how to handle mine."

I stomped through the kitchen and slammed back out through the screen door. The star jasmine vines curled away from my feet. The tall grass swept back as if I were a wind. How dare he! A husband! Gods! Like I needed a man to control me. Like I couldn't be a competent sorceress on my own.

"Pig!" I snarled. I clenched my fists and sent magic spurting through my fingers. I wanted to see something shrivel to a blackened crisp so I could pretend it was Zeusse.

A bombshell of yellow and white butterflies exploded out of the bindweed growing in the roadside ditch. Not at all satisfying.

Okay, yes, fine. I was nineteen and still a virgin. Some people might be ashamed of that, but the way I looked at it, I was picky.

Let's face it: I look good. That's not conceit, it's just fact, and Mom's always said that false modesty is just vanity dressed up in socially acceptable garb. The point is, I had my share of admirers. More than my share, some might say. Some I liked all right, but none enough to get hot and heavy with. In fact, none I felt confident who weren't just after the obvious. And I wasn't about to do something I didn't feel like doing just to erase the dreaded "V" word off my résumé.

But to have Zeusse going all paternalistic on me because of it, not to mention him thinking he knew what I did (or didn't do) with my spare time—ugh. I suddenly wished I'd been wearing a pair of baggy sweats. And that still didn't entirely explain why I was so angry.

I threw myself into my car and slammed the door. That wasn't very satisfying, either, because I drove a twenty-year-old Toyota and the door sounded like banging an empty tomato can on the kitchen counter. The engine wasn't powerful enough to spin the tires, so the angriest-sounding thing I could do was wind it up real good before shifting to the next gear.

I hit the road in front of our house, a two-lane farm road as straight as the people around there. A field of bell peppers stretched away on one side, eggplant on the other, the rows of dark green leaves flickering by. Monocrops as monotonous as the Valley itself, about as soothing as a song sung on one note.

After ten years living in the hills of northern California's Coast Range, in the little, golden coastal valleys with their oaks and rows of grapevines, we'd moved to the Central Valley. All that agriculture, you know, *and* a long growing season. Mom could be blissfully busy encouraging the crops to produce their best for nine months out of the year and break up the routine by doing fertility magic and midwifery for the farm laborers' wives and touring dairies to boost the milk output.

Me, I hated the Valley. It was flat. It was boring. It was foggy for weeks on end in the wintertime and hotter than…well, Hell in the summer, and it had this weird sort of pungent smell, something compounded of fertilizer and manure and rotting cornstalks and stuff left over in the fields after harvesting.

And talk about un-magical. Mom could go around doing the most blatant magic and *nobody* caught on but the field workers.

At times like these, it felt like every problem I had came from the Valley, and if I didn't get away, I'd explode.

Damn, Zeusse, anyway. Why did he have to act like some kind of patriarch just because my dad, whoever he was, was nowhere in the picture…

Oh, crap. And if Zeusse acted like that with Mom, what did he think he could do with *me?*

What argument had I interrupted, anyway? And why was Mom so mad? I shuddered. Zeusse might be more determined to get me married than I knew.

I headed for the hills, my childhood home, my place of comfort. To the west, the land swelled like ripples of honey. Winding into the hills, the road narrowed, a grey ribbon tracing the creases between. Round, steep slopes pied dark green with oaks rose all around. I was sheltered there. Alone, for the most part. I pulled off the road, cut the engine and climbed out of the car.

A little thread of green down to the right hinted at a spring-fed rivulet. More oaks, grand, twisted and ageless, leaned across it like giants whispering secrets. A meadowlark sang somewhere. A breeze gossiped in the grass. I should have felt better, but I wouldn't have been able to tell you which churned more, my guts or my brain.

I walked toward the trees a few yards off the road, and the grass went from gossiping to thrashing. I dropped to the ground under the oaks, flung myself on my back and looked up. The black, gnarled branches clattered, raining leaves and green acorns down on me, but what was I supposed to do? I suppose it would've been kinder to take my bad attitude to a parking lot somewhere, but then I'd've had to watch people frantically piling into backseats.

So I just lay there, staring up at the wispy streaks of mare's tails against the blue and listening to the poor oaks crack and groan in more growth than they'd put on in the last fifty years. I imagined rolling up my power like a garden hose, trying to make it something tidy and fully in my control, but it kept rearing up and squirting my mind's eye. And then something changed.

I didn't know what it was, at first. It was like falling asleep in the shade only to suddenly wake sweating in full sun. I shot up, hands braced behind me.

A woman was walking toward me. She was round and brown with hair the color of a waterfall's plume cascading down her back. Her dress looked like it was woven of grass, and she wore a basketry cap and ropes of necklaces made of seeds. *Yokuts Indian* popped into my mind, from a picture I'd seen in some book, then the sorceress in me woke up and said, *Um, no, I don't think so.*

Sometimes with really powerful sorcerers, the magic grows so strong they almost become emanations, embodiments, if you will, of the magic. This woman was so powerful I wasn't sure if she was even corporeal. Yes, she had a shape I could see and feet (clad in shoes made of woven rushes) that brushed though the grass. But looking into her eyes was like looking up into a moonless night sky way up in the mountains: black and deep as infinity.

Somewhere between the moment I saw her and the time it took her to cross the few yards to my tree, I'd scrambled to my feet. She was shorter than me, but that didn't diminish her in the least.

She looked up into the moaning, distressed oaks. "You're troubled, Kore, and troubling things." Her voice was like a whisper of flame, soft and rich.

*Kore?* Why did she call me that? "I—I'm sorry," I said. It was pitiful, but I couldn't think of anything else. And whoever this lady was, I was pretty sure I didn't want to piss her off.

She considered me. A breeze wound around her like an affectionate cat, lifting her white hair over one shoulder, tickling her face with its ends.

"Come," she said at last. "Let us take your trouble elsewhere and let these, my other children, grow in peace."

I swallowed once. Or tried to, anyway, brushing leaves and an acorn cap out of my hair. "Okay."

I wasn't about to argue. Earth sorcerers don't like people messing with their charges—I knew that from Mom. And this one made my mom look like a birthday party magician.

The world turned...sort of translucent, I guess, then foggy, or blurry, and then it gradually faded into somewhere else. Actually, *somewhere* isn't quite accurate, since I suspect it was another dimension, some plane where magic is a purer force than it is in the so-called real world. The sorceress beside me no longer looked like an Indian woman. She looked like a goddess, with earth-colored skin, starlight hair, a dress of rain, blouse of clouds and cloak of wind. She glowed like a sleepy volcano with the fires of her power. Her eyes, though, remained as I'd seen them, night-dark and deep.

She glanced aside at me. I think she was watching to see how I took the translocation. I'm not sure what she saw, but I felt small and tacky.

"You're Demetra's daughter."

This was not a question, but I nodded unnecessarily.

"Young," she said. "Very young." She said it like a mother speaking of her homely child.

I gave a rueful shrug.

"Hmm." She began walking.

This place—plane, whatever—was similar to what I'd just left, except that the grass we walked through was the essence of grass, the hills the souls of hills, not quite so solid-looking and more glowy. The oaks gazed down on us with slow, ancient awareness. I hunched my shoulders and thought *Sorry!* at them.

As we went, the trees began to look more like columns, the grass more like a floor, the hills like walls. Even growing up in a sorcerous family, this was strange, let me tell you. It was stranger still because the house seemed to have a consciousness, and it was aware of me.

"Um," I said, "where are we going, Ma'am?" I really wanted to ask, *What are you going to do with me?* but this seemed neither particularly diplomatic nor something I really wanted to know.

She smiled as if she knew exactly what I hadn't asked. "To my workshop. It's accustomed to containing great power."

Oh. Or was it uh-oh?

"What does your mother call you?" she asked.

"Perry—Persephonie, when I'm in trouble."

"Persephonie," she said, smiling again. "I am Gaia."

*Gaia?* Oh, gods. The Earth Mother. Even I knew her by reputation, no matter that Mom and I almost never hung around other sorcerers. And she'd called me Persephonie. But I didn't need that to tell me I was in big trouble. I'd been spouting off power for three months or so. So what had I finally done that was so awful she'd decided to put in an appearance?

"So, why do you leave your mother's dominion to come troubling mine?"

"I—oh—well…" I started to point at the columns

that had been tormented oak trees a few minutes ago, but since they were now pillars of black marble with green veining, threw up my hands instead. "You saw. No, it's more than that. My uncle seems to think—" I glanced at her. I really hated spilling the tawdry particulars of our little family spat.

"Your uncle Zeusse? A great practitioner of sex magic." She gazed at me politely—and shrewdly. "And one who tends to think in such terms."

There was no particular reason my face should go hot at this comment, nevertheless it did. "Exactly." I looked down at the green and brown and gold tiles passing under my feet. They looked strangely like an aerial view of the Valley and hills, but without roads or buildings. "I don't think my magic is dependent on that."

She cocked her head to the side. "Are you so sure what your magic is and is not?"

It was patently obvious I didn't. So what was she saying? That Zeusse was right?

I shrugged. "I guess I don't want someone telling me. I need to find out for myself."

"Yes," she said with a single, firm nod.

Although that should have been encouraging, I was alarmed. Well, more alarmed, I should say. It wasn't as if I could excuse myself, return to my car and drive home if I felt like it. And what, exactly, was supposed to take place in this workshop that could contain great powers?

So I'd pretty much worked myself up to the point

where I was sick to my stomach by the time Gaia stopped in front of a door. It was carved, and the copper nails and bindings were so old they'd turned green and bled darkish, greenish streaks down the wood.

"Here we are," she said.

I eyed the door. Would I find behind it a great cauldron in which she stirred the climate? Or maybe a computer where she ran simulations of entire ecosystems? Maybe the room would be empty except for a comfortable chair where she sat when she linked psychically with the world organism, brain to its body.

The door swung open on a sigh of hinges.

The place looked like a cross between a zoo and a huge potting shed. The walls alternated wicker cages with slatted benches. A microscope and small chemistry lab complete with beakers, test tubes and flasks stood atop glossy wood cabinets in a little alcove. If this was her workshop, she was a real workaholic. But this was the quintessential earth sorceress, too. According to Mom, maybe the oldest and most powerful in the world.

The cages were all empty, as were most of the potting benches, except for a few plants clustered together off to one side: azaleas, oleander, gardenia, lily, a rose and an iris, all white. They made a couple of exotic-looking house plants with dark, almost black leaves look somber and standoffish by comparison. Since my emotional state was anything but tranquil, the plants all kind of rustled, like elegant ladies at a tea party where someone just fumbled a cup.

Gaia extended a plump, brown hand. "I would like you to work with these."

I looked across the hangar-like expanse of workshop at the huddle of plants. They seemed to stare warily back.

"Work?" What was I supposed to do? More to the point, why?

"I wish to create a hybrid," she explained and gestured as if sketching a vision. "I see black foliage nicely setting off white flowers."

I looked at the plants — different species. Hell, even a few different genera — then back at her. "Um…"

Gathering some little camel hair brushes from a drawer, she smiled. "You are an earth sorceress, are you not?"

I sighed silently. "I'm a make-everything-insanely-fruitful sorceress, as far as I can tell." Beloved at the nursery where I worked for starts and transplants, but the gods knew what would happen if I tried to get fancy.

She handed me the brushes, smiling implacably. "Indulge me."

I took them and said, "Yes, Ma'am." Hey, would *you* argue with a sorceress so steeped in magic she was halfway to becoming a goddess?

The plants, of course, proved to be happy to do as I asked, unfurling perfect flowers. Even the black-leaved houseplants did, although their flowers were tiny and pale and waxy-looking, like grubs or baby moles. I dabbed pollen from stamens and brushed it onto pistils, while Gaia wrote on little tags and covered the fertilized flowers with clear plastic bags.

I won't go into the minutiae of propagation. Leave it to say that we soon had several flats of black-green sprouts. I potted them as fast as I could, and when I finished the last ones, the first were in bloom, all black-leaved with clear white flowers, naturally, since that was what I'd wanted.

Gaia studied them, examining leaves and sniffing flowers. I stood behind her, nibbling on a thumbnail and shifting my weight.

What was the point of all this? Maybe she was testing me somehow, trying to find if I was worth the trouble after all the havoc I'd caused. If not—what? Would she take me home and impose upon Mom to take some serious steps to rein me in? Or worse, did she herself have something in mind?

She stepped back and turned to me. "Choose the best."

Best? Best for what? Hardiness? Vigor? Beauty? Or maybe the question had nothing to do with any of that. Maybe it was another test.

I looked them over with both ordinary and magical perception. It was hard to choose since I'd made them myself, albeit under worrisome circumstances. I settled on a lush, tropical-looking rosette of long, tongue-shaped leaves with irisy flowers.

She gave me an indecipherable, sidelong look. "Yes? Why?"

"Well…" I shifted my weight again and brushed invisible specks of potting mix off my hands. "I think it's the prettiest, and…"

"And?"

"It just wants to *be*. It's full of life and…" I gestured, searching for words to explain.

"Love?" she offered.

Love, hmm. Was that it? The plant felt to me like a lamp in the darkness, like no matter what happened, it would continue to shine. But love? I wasn't sure about that. I shrugged.

She turned, caressing a white, ruffled petal with a strong finger. "What does your mother say of your magic?"

"Not much." I pulled a rose petal off the bush beside me, rubbed it between my fingers. It felt like moist silk. "I think she's worried, though." I breathed in the rose fragrance, a smell like spice and citrus and rain. "*I'm* worried."

I'd been worried about so many things lately the admission just popped out. I held the pale petal to my nose and breathed. Gaia didn't say anything, and her silence began to feel like someone who is reluctant to speak an unpleasant truth.

"It's not like we haven't been trying to—to control it, you know—Mom and I." I threw up my hands. "It's like owning this huge, exuberant Great Dane puppy, and every time I try to take it out somewhere, it goes lunging off, dragging me along on the other end of the leash."

To my utter humiliation, tears started in my eyes. Boo-hoo. Poor little Perry, bursting with uncontrollable impulses like some angst-ridden adolescent. I sniffed and cleared my throat.

Gaia cupped the flower in one hand as if it were a tear-streaked face. Letting her hand fall, she turned. "You make things grow and bloom, do you not?"

I nodded, swallowing. My throat still felt achy and threatening.

"Perhaps," she said, "your difficulty lies in that you haven't yet found the proper subject. Perhaps, rather than struggling against what you contain, you should search for its purpose."

I wasn't sure whether to fall to my knees in gratitude or supplication: the former because it sounded like she wasn't planning anything dreadful for me after all, the latter because she might know what I had to do but wasn't planning to tell me.

## II

I wasn't quite sure what to make of my little adventure in the hills. Gaia put me back where I belonged, but why had she whisked me away to her realm to begin with? Surely not to do something she could have done, except better and with less fuss.

Need I say I didn't tell Mom? Not that we tend to keep things from one another, but if she knew I'd disturbed the Big Gun of earth sorceresses, she might be inclined to drastic measures—like listening to Uncle Zeusse.

No thanks.

I was in the kitchen fixing us pepper jack cheese sandwiches on bagels with cucumber, sprouts and Dijon mustard when someone knocked. Mom, stirring sugar into fresh-squeezed lemonade, left the spoon in the pitcher and went to answer the door.

Zeusse' big, booming voice came from the front room.

Ugh. He'd just been here a couple of weeks ago. At least this time I was wearing a t-shirt and green overalls, my work clothes.

I cut the sandwiches in half, put them on plates, finished stirring the sugar into the lemonade and poured. Two plates, two glasses. I did *not* want to encourage Zeusse to stay. Besides, he's more of a spareribs and baked potato sort of guy.

"Perry," Mom called from the front room.

That was strange. Usually Zeusse just imposed his way on in. Gods forbid he should allow himself to be invited to join us for lunch like anyone else. I put our sandwiches on the table.

"Coming, Mom."

I thought about stalling by putting the lemonade in the fridge and wiping the counter, but that would look like tidying up for Zeusse's benefit. So I just wiped my hands and went out.

Zeusse was dressed in a sky-blue polo shirt, new jeans and boots. Someone else stood in the space between the open door and the window, where the glare from outside made it hard to see, but I was more curious about Zeusse' upgraded attire.

He extended a big, blunt hand toward me and said, "This is my niece, Persephonie. Perry, meet Aros."

The someone stepped forward, and a hand captured mine. "Hi," he said, shaking my hand. "Pleased to meet you, Persephonie."

"Perry," I said automatically. I had an impression of tallness and fairness, then my brain came back online.

He was tall, all right—about Zeusse' height without the bulk, with grey-blue eyes and an engaging lopsided grin on a tanned face. His hair was the color of good-quality beer and he was good-looking. *Wow.* Was he ever good-looking. The archetypical Surfer Guy. He must've been cranking out pheromones or something because I just stood there shaking his hand like I was priming a pump.

"Hi!" I said, and my voice sounded like a middle-school girl's, all bright and breathless. "We were just having lunch. Would you like some?"

Mom's brows rose.

"That sounds wonderful," Zeusse said, shooting Mom a look. At the moment, though, I wasn't paying much attention.

"We wouldn't want to impose…" Aros said.

He broke eye contact for a questioning glance at Zeusse and my mom, and I abruptly recognized that look on Zeusse's face: smugness.

Mom made gracious noises and ushered the men into the kitchen. She got two more glasses out of the cupboard and poured lemonade. I opened the fridge. Half my attention was on rattling off lunch choices like the waitress at the diner down by the railroad tracks while the other half seethed about that smug look.

The contents of the refrigerator weren't nearly as distracting as Aros. Possibilities were beginning to occur to me. I carried lettuce and a tomato to the sink and began washing them.

"What do you do, Aros?" Mom said.

"I'm a student right now." His voice was almost as distracting as his face. I concentrated on his words.

"And what are you studying?"

She might have asked, 'Who are you studying

with?' since neither one of us could miss the fact that he was a sorcerer. But believe it or not, sorcerers go to everyday, garden-variety school like I had, so the question wasn't unreasonable.

"Are you working today, Perry?" Zeusse said loudly, but not loudly enough that I missed Aros' answer:

"I'm studying with Zeusse."

My hands under the tapwater froze on the lettuce leaf. My guts, on the other hand, cranked up to *Incinerate*. The lettuce leaf sprouted suddenly into a whole head and the tomato produced six or seven pups, like a succulent.

There was silence behind me, but my ears buzzed like someone had whacked a hornet's nest in my head. I dropped the lettuce in the sink, shut off the tap and turned.

I looked at Zeusse. If my magic worked that way, *he* might've been sprouting pups or extra heads. The silence seemed to stretch on and on, though it was probably only a second or two.

"Work today?" I said to him. "Yep. In fact, I gotta go." Drying my hands on a dishtowel, I turned to Aros. "Glad to have met you. Good luck with your studies," I added in my usual sunshine-and-daisies voice.

I tossed the dishtowel onto the counter and walked out.

I stomped into the nursery awhile later, although the drive from the house hadn't taken as long as usual. At this rate, I was going to blow a rod in my poor old Toyota.

Henry Asakawa, the owner, was at the counter ringing up a middle-aged lady's purchases: hot-pink and lavender crepe myrtles, heavenly bamboo and some ajuga. A couple of housewives conferred over the pinks.

Eleanor, one of my coworkers, was tidying wisteria plants in the Vines section. She looked up. "Hey, Perry."

"Hey," I said. The honeysuckles were furtively winding vines around one another, creeping themselves upward like wrestling snakes. I hurried past before Eleanor could notice.

"Aren't you early?" she called.

"A little," I called back and ducked into the back section, where the young plants were hardened off.

The ones nearest me put on two or three months' growth before I made it into the greenhouse. At the potting bench, I pulled a stack of plastic six-pack containers and a bag of seed-starting medium from under the bench.

Eleanor came in behind me. She was twenty-two and had worked in the nursery since she was eighteen, gotten a degree in ornamental horticulture from MJC in the meantime and was starting her landscape design business.

Most of the young people working at Zen Gardens were just there for the after-school bucks, but Eleanor and I were true disciples. Barring sorcery, we had a lot in common.

"A little early, huh?" she said. "How about two hours?"

I scooped seed-starting medium into the containers. "Yeah, well."

She leaned against a support beam. "What's the matter? Tell Auntie Ellie."

"Nothing you can help with." Unless she knew a hit man who specialized in sorcerers.

I scanned the list of stuff Henry wanted started: sunflowers, marigolds, moss rose, verbena: the kind of thing that tolerated the hot, dry Valley summers.

She studied me. "It must be gruesome, since you're not your usual sweet, mild self."

I jabbed holes in the medium with a dowel. "My uncle's trying to marry me off. He brought a prospective bridegroom to inspect the goods just now."

Her brows shot up like Mom's had. "My, how Middle Eastern. Was he very awful, balding and with red and blue veins mapping his nose, or perhaps young with thick glasses and a protrudent Adam's apple?"

I made a disgusted noise. "He was young and polite and looked like a movie star. His voice would melt chocolate."

"Hmm." She nodded thoughtfully. "And the problem is?"

"He's too pretty for my taste," I grumbled.

"Oh, yes. That kind of thing is always a deal-breaker."

I rounded on her. "Hey, I'll tell you what. I'll tell my uncle my best friend is also single, and he can work on arranging a marriage for *you*. If the guy he brings around decides you'll do, I'll go to the wedding and throw rice."

Eleanor held up her hands. "Okay! I was just trying to put a positive spin on the situation. You were the one who painted the scrumptious picture."

"Yeah. Well, thanks."

She came and leaned beside me. "Is it really that bad?"

I nodded. "You'd think I could decide when and who I want to marry, wouldn't you?"

She looked shocked. Apparently she thought I'd been exaggerating. Maybe I'd told her too many horror stories about Zeusse.

"Jesus, Perry. Why don't you leave home? You're over eighteen. You don't have to put up with crap like that."

That was oddly comforting, although it didn't change anything.

I shrugged. "I like living with my mom. We get along really well. And we'd miss each other if we were apart."

She shook her head, took a few plastic six-packs and started slowly filling one. "So what happened?"

"Zeusse brings this guy in, I spend the first ten minutes drooling and batting my eyelashes, then see the look on my uncle's face and realize what's going on."

"And then?"

I poked marigold seeds into the little holes I'd made. *Please*, I thought, *don't pop up yet. Wait until tomorrow, at least.* "I left my lunch sitting on the kitchen table, grabbed my car keys and came here."

Eleanor stared at me. "You didn't even talk to him?"

"Before I came to my senses, I asked him to stay for lunch."

"Perry!"

"What?"

"You ask the poor guy to stay for lunch and then leave?"

"Well..." Looked at in that light, it was pretty inexcusable. I thought of Aros' lopsided grin while he shook my hand, his abashed look as I stalked out, the silence in the kitchen as I shoved through the door. "They shouldn't have sprung him on me like that, then."

"What did they say? 'Here's your future husband, Perry. Give him a kiss and let's figure out where to seat the guests.'"

I smoothed medium over the seeds with my thumb. "No..." My t-shirt suddenly felt itchy, especially under the arms and around the collar.

She leaned an elbow on the bench. "Your face is red."

"Maybe I overreacted a little. Nothing I can do

about it now."

She raised her brows.

I banged the scoop I'd been using on the bench. "If I go home and apologize, Zeusse will think he's won. It'll be ten times worse."

A man's voice said from the greenhouse door, "I was going to let you buy me out on good terms when I retire, but now I see you two standing there yakking like the rest of the kids, I'm not so sure."

Eleanor and I both turned. Henry stood in the doorway, his short white hair bristling like shorn dry grass in the sunlight, an arch look on his round face.

Henry was actually a fantastic boss if you loved plants and were willing to work. If you did, he'd answer all your questions, show you how to do anything you asked and pretty much leave you alone and let you do your job. Those who treated the nursery like a big backyard in which to squirt hoses at coworkers and find shady places to sleep also thought he was a great guy—until they found themselves standing on the sidewalk with their final checks in their hands.

"I'm not on the clock yet, Henry," I said.

"Then what're you doing here, distracting my employees?"

"Working," I replied the same time Eleanor said, "She's hiding out."

Looking from one to the other of us, he said, "Uh-huh."

"But see," I said cheerfully, "it's okay for Eleanor

to stand here talking to me because I'm working for free to make up for it."

"Sure," he said, nodding. "As long as you two got nothing to do, come with me." He turned and disappeared from the doorway.

Eleanor gave me an alarmed look. I wasn't feeling optimistic, either, but that might have been leftover guilty conscience from the subject of our interrupted conversation.

Henry wasn't waiting. As he passed the mugo pines, he called to Ryle to keep an eye on things for a few minutes. Ryle, watering the ferns, nodded and walked over to shut off the water. When he saw Eleanor and me slinking after Henry, he turned his hands palm up: *What's up?* I shrugged, Eleanor flapped a hand at him and we both stepped into the store.

The shelves of garden tools and seeds and pots stood ranked like clay statues of soldiers in a Chinese tomb. Wind chimes tinkled in the breeze that came through the open door. The faint, pungent scents of fertilizer and weed killer curled around me. I didn't see Henry anywhere, but his office door was open, so I knew he was in there. We walked in, and Eleanor shut the door. Pessimist.

He gave her a funny look, one I couldn't quite figure out. It might have been amusement or puzzlement or wickedness, of some combination thereof. He sat down and as usual, his chair gave an agonized squeak. Eleanor and I stood in front of his desk like kids sent to the principal's office.

He rummaged around in a pile of bills, advertisements and order forms, grunted and pulled out a card.

It was about the size and shape of a formal invitation, parchment brown with a trimming of green foil. Apparently thinking it was a Go to the Unemployment Line card, Eleanor could only stare at it, so I took it.

Large, ornate letters said,

## Plant Show
### Palace Suites Hotel, Modesto, California
### Friday, August 26

*You are cordially invited to an event hosted by California's most exclusive hybridizer, TerraVisions. Please join us for a very special debut of our newest cultivars, specimens guaranteed to intrigue the most discriminating gardener.*
*This will be a semi-formal occasion complete with hors d'oeuvres and a full-host bar.*
*Please RSVP to Gay Cosimia of TerraVisions by July 9*

Eleanor was anxiously reading over my shoulder.

We looked at each other, then at Henry.

One side of his mouth quirked in a half-repressed smile. "I was planning on sending you two, 'cause I figured you'd look a lot better in monkey clothes than me. But now—"

"Is this the part where we're supposed to beg?" I clutched the invitation to my breast. "Please, Henry, please let us go. I'll stand in the middle of the nursery and murmur encouraging words to the plants all day." He was always teasing me about how much better the plants grew when I was around. Ha ha.

"I'll scrub the whole pile of used containers with bleach water," Eleanor added.

Ooh. That one was hard to top. Bleach water did terrible things to your hands. "I'll replace the broken lathe over the hostas," I said.

"I'll—" Eleanor began, but Henry laughed and waved his hands in surrender.

"Okay, okay. Next you'll be promising me free labor for a year."

"Not me," Eleanor said. "I have to pay rent."

Henry looked at me.

Uh-oh. Time to change the subject. I put on my best oblivious look. "So why do you want to send us?"

He leveled a finger. "It's time you girls learn the buying side of the business. That part's just as important as the customers and the plants, 'cause if you don't have what people want, you're not gonna stay in business long."

"Right, Henry," we said meekly.

Eleanor's eyes were wide and dreamy. Visions of blue roses, red wisteria and white marigolds flitted through my imagination, so I probably looked much the same. With everything going on in my life at the moment, it was as if a miserable Valley winter fog had wisped away to let the clear sunlight pour down.

ഇ

It would be nice to be able to say that everything unfortunate and difficult had been wiped away with that single piece of glowing news. But the fact remained that in addition to still splattering magic everywhere like gore in a slasher film, I'd been Bad, Rude and Generally Unpleasant. Every time I thought about the dismay on Aros' good-looking (if somewhat too pretty) face, I cringed. Okay, yes, he was Zeusse's student, but it didn't necessarily follow that he had to assume Zeusse's attitudes. This is, after all, the twenty-first century. Even sorcerers have to adapt to the times.

The mature thing would've been to call Aros and apologize. I didn't. I dithered. I made excuses to myself. I rationalized that all the *sturm und drang* was in my own head, and he'd probably only seen a woman who had to hurry up and get to work. If I did bring it up, it would cause more embarrassment than if I'd left the matter alone. Worse still, it might look like some kind of overture of romantic interest.

The two months leading up to the Plant Show

went by in this fashion. The day—or afternoon, rather—finally arrived, and although I was no closer to dealing with the consequences of my behavior, I was perfectly happy to forget about them for the moment.

Eleanor pulled up in her pickup and got out, clad in a halter-top dress with a handkerchief skirt in hues of aqua and lavender. She wore a necklace and earrings set with small, round moonstones and mother-of-pearl. Climbing out of that truck, she looked like contradiction personified.

Mom had helped me with my hair. I usually just tied it back in a ponytail, but now it was piled up on my head with a few alluring wisps loose on my cheeks and neck.

We stood and oohed and ahhed over each other's clothes and jewelry and hair, then I kissed Mom goodbye, hitched up my skirt and clambered into Eleanor's truck.

Modesto seemed enormous to me since Mom had never been one for cities, even small ones. Highway 99 with its iceplant and oleander, its cloverleaf on and offramps, wasn't terribly foreign, but the hotel—my gosh, ten stories or so!—was amazing. The inside was indeed like a palace, the marble floors, the reception desk with its brass trim and uniformed staff.

We made our way along a gallery the width of a narrow street to open double doors. The room within was filled with men in dark suits, women in as many kinds of dresses as there are flowers in a meadow.

The murmur of conversation, the chime of laughter, the clink of glasses wove, curiously, throughout the splashing of water. We threaded our way through the logjam of people near the doors and the room opened ahead.

A demure little fountain played in the center of the room under a round skylight. It was still early enough that soft evening light filtered through, bathing the fountain, the circle of tile and the people around it in undersea hues. And plants were everywhere, along the walls, surrounding the fountain, hanging from the ceiling, standing among the guests like well-behaved children.

"Wow," Eleanor breathed.

I just nodded. We drifted toward the nearest plant, something that looked like a bougainvillea except the bracts were gold as coins and the leaves were watermelon-striped green and white, but something else snared my attention.

Magic. I stopped and looked. Another sorcerer was here—no, several sorcerers. The longer I looked around, the more I saw. Not as many as there were regular people, of course, but more than a handful. Weird.

Eleanor was looking back at me. "What's wrong?"

*I thought I recognized someone,* I started to say, since I obviously couldn't tell the truth. If I'd only turned around, I could've said it with perfect honesty.

Someone put a hand on my shoulder and said, "Hey, Perry."

I turned, and there was Aros.

I came this close to blurting out, *What're you doing here?* Fortunately, I didn't, and bit my lip to make sure it stayed that way. He was nicely dressed in a navy blue jacket and beige slacks.

He apparently mistook my consternation for puzzlement, because he said, "Remember me? Aros."

"Aros, yes, hi," I said weakly.

Oh, gods. I was getting hot from my armpits all the way to my hairline. And violent red would definitely not go with my ensemble. I glanced around like a cornered criminal.

It only got worse. With my distressed emotional state, my already tenuous grip on magic was slipping. Eleanor was looking at Aros with unseemly interest.

"Eleanor," I said. "This is Aros, my uncle's student." I couldn't just disappear him without some kind of introduction. It would look weird. No, it would look like I wanted him to myself—I mean, *for* myself. And Eleanor was too good a friend to make her feel that way. "Will you excuse us for a minute?"

She only gazed at Aros like a comet being pulled into the sun. The people within my immediate proximity were all gravitating toward nearby members of the opposite sex—and a few to the same sex.

I knew I should have made that phone call to Aros, and now I was going to have to humiliate myself without the proper loin-girding.

I put on a smile, pretended half the room wasn't

about to ravish the other half and asked him, "Can we talk?"

His brows quirked, but he still smiled. "Of course."

I grabbed his hand, towed him out of the room and down the hallway. To the right, a door opened to the outside. I pushed through, out onto a patio. The lights in the pool nearby sent ripples of green light shivering across the surrounding walls.

Releasing Aros' hand, I walked to the patio, found a couple of chairs and sat down. He sat too, looking concerned.

"I'm really sorry about that." I dropped my head in my hand. This was not beginning well. "That is, I owe you an apology." He opened his mouth to say something, but if I was going to do it, I had to get it over with then. "I was rude. At my mother's house. You didn't deserve that." There. I would have let out a breath, but I'd already run out of air saying all that in a rush.

Now he looked serious. "I did sense some tension."

"It was nothing to do with you." Or at least not directly.

Lacing his fingers, he glanced down. "I appreciate that. But…I had the sense that it *was* me."

What could I say? It depended if he was in collusion with my uncle's plots?

I sighed. "It's…" His face still wore that expression of gentle concern. And after all, he had eyes. Surely he'd seen what happened back in the room. "It's just that my magic tends to be a little…" I gestured, euphemisms having failed me for the moment.

"Vigorous?" he offered.

"Something like that. And Zeusse—" There was a lot I could say on the subject. However, I needed to remember that this man was his pupil. "Well, he has his ideas, and he's very set on them."

Aros laughed. "He is, isn't he?"

A little smile tugged at my lips. Maybe in spite of his pretty-boy, pop-god looks, Aros was all right. So often people who look like him tend to forget they need to be decent human beings, too. And it would be a shame to have to despise him.

"I'm afraid so," I replied.

"But listen," he said, "seriously, there is something you can do about…your problem."

I tensed. "Oh yeah?"

He glanced around the patio. Except for the two of us, it was empty, just the glowing green water rippling softly in the dimness, the lonely chairs and tables and chaise lounges.

He stood and held out a hand. "Here, give me your hand."

I eyed him. "Why?"

"I want to show you something. Come on. It's nothing terrible."

Of course, if I didn't, I'd look like an idiot. So I gave him my hand. He pulled me to my feet.

"Now," he said and raised his other hand. "Ready?"

I suppose I could have said something about abandoning my friend so abruptly, or that this wasn't the time and place to be trying magic. I could even have simply said "No," but social propriety can put one in all kinds of difficult positions.

His hand was level with my head. While I stood there trying to figure out how to get out of my predicament, he slipped it around behind my head and pulled me to him.

And kissed me.

Now, let me explain that Aros' magic is not inconsiderable. Nor are other sorcerers necessarily immune to it. And his magic happens to be *really good* for this kind of thing.

All of which goes a long way toward explaining why I just stood there for some indeterminate amount of time, more or less gradually turning into a pair of lips with a body attached. It had almost gotten to the point where other, tenderer parts would begin to respond when I thought, *Hey, wait a minute. Going pretty* fast *here, aren't we?*

I tried to pull away, but he locked my head in the crook of one arm and clamped his other hand on my butt. This, however, did not have the desired effect of convincing me to succumb to his male prowess or whatever. I started struggling in earnest, and the bastard *bit my lip*.

I was furious. And truth be known, not a little

scared. If I'd been able to think about it, I could've used magic on him. A little burst of what *I* can do, and his intestinal flora or the bacteria living on his skin would've experienced a sudden population explosion. The resulting prurient rash (no pun intended) or expulsion of bodily fluids from both ends would have dissuaded him admirably.

But under the circumstances, I did what comes naturally: I kneed him.

I found myself standing free while he snarled obscenities and clutched something rather more important to him than I was. I paused long enough to finger my poor lip and spit a few choice cusswords of my own. Then I bolted.

I not-quite ran down the corridor, my long, full skirt tangling around my legs. My heart galloped, and my lip was throbbing on the offbeats like the tuba bass line in a marching band — *oomp-oomp*. I touched it again — it didn't feel like it was bleeding, but did feel puffy.

Damn him! What if it started showing a bruise? Wisps of hair flew around my face and brushed my shoulders, and my hands shook when I tried to stuff the loose bits back up into my hairdo. At last, I spotted the ladies' room. The perfect sanctuary. I dived inside.

I definitely couldn't return to the Plant Show in my present condition. Even after I'd applied copious amounts of cold water to my lip, repaired my hair and straightened my clothes, it was a while before I felt reasonably sure that my entrance wouldn't instantly turn the room into a jungle full of sighing and moaning couples.

It did cross my mind to leave a message for Eleanor and call Mom to come get me, but dammit! I'd come to see the plants. I *wanted* to see the plants. Why should I let Aros send me scampering home like a scared puppy?

So I took a long breath, looked in the mirror again to make sure my lip wasn't showing any visible damage and marched out of the bathroom. (Actually, I cracked the door open and peeked through first. *Then* I marched out.)

The Plant Show's enormous room was even fuller than when I'd left it. The sound of voices filled the space like the drone of crickets on a summer night. And what was with all these sorcerers? Magic hazed the air, buzzed against my skin, chirped and hummed and sang. I didn't recognize any faces, but that wasn't surprising. Mom preferred to spend her time helping regular people.

I searched for Eleanor for a while without success, then decided we'd bump into one another sooner or later. Plus it was getting harder to walk past all those fantastic plants.

I drifted to magenta irises edged in gold to roses with the fragrance of orange blossoms. I drooled over apple trees bearing fruit like carved ivory spheres. Crowds gathered around the showiest plants, like the one hanging above the fountain. It had to be a fuchsia of some kind, although the leaves were purplely-green and its flowers sported orange sepals with a creamy yellow corona. It looked like a sunset.

I moved before it had a chance to grow noticeably, meandering my way toward the quieter fringes. Here plants stood in little alcoves lit with spots and accompanied by black nameplates, like the works of art they were. And like avant-garde art, they drew only a few people to silently admire their charms. The sword-leaved thing with spidery, dark maroon flowers. A plant that looked like a contorted old troll with a spray of twisted grass for hair. A succulent like a pile of rocks.

Of course, I was one of the die-hards, walking from one to the next with absorbed contentment and delight until a jolt of some seriously powerful magic buffeted me from the side. Startled—(No, I have to be honest here. A bolt of panic went through me.)—my head snapped around.

A few feet away, a man stood alone in a little cul-de-sac before another plant of which I could only see tips of dark leaves. His back was to me, showing a tall, broad-shouldered form in a black suit, meticulously groomed black hair skimming the collar.

I relaxed. He was a sorcerer, obviously, but not Aros, and that was enough to keep me from ducking for the nearest source of cover. In fact, the odd...*straining* of magic, as if something was blocking or interfering with it in some way, made me curious.

For some few moments, he just stood looking (I

supposed) at the plant. At last, he raised his hand to it. His fingers, outstretched, hung inches from the leaves...then fell to his side again without touching them.

It was such a despairing, lonely gesture, I half wanted to slip away to give the poor guy some privacy, half wanted to ask him if he was okay. Then he moved slightly and I saw the plant he was looking at.

Have you ever had the experience of seeing someone you know out of context? Like a casual acquaintance at the grocery store, and you know you've seen them somewhere before but doggoned if you can remember where.

Seeing the plant sitting there on its little pedestal in that spotlighted alcove was like that. It was about the general size of a hybrid tea rosebush, its foot-long, black-velvet leaves springing upward in a graceful fountain, a crown of clear white ruffled flowers floating like gleaming drops on their tall stalks.

It was my plant. The one Gaia had asked me to create.

I gave a little "Oh!" of surprise, and the man turned.

I would say he spun, except the movement was too controlled for that. But it was quick, and he caught me staring.

He was as good-looking as Aros, in a dark, stern sort of way, with a neatly-trimmed beard and mustache. Older, I guessed, but not as old as Zeusse.

And his eyes—the Phantom of the Opera must've had eyes like that. Rasputin. Svengali. I was looking right into them from a distance of no more than six feet and couldn't tell you what color they were, only that I couldn't look away.

It began to dimly occur to me that I was being rude again, on several fronts.

"Oh," I said again and blinked. "I—um—didn't mean to...disturb you."

He stood still, and for a second I thought he would just walk away. I wouldn't have blamed him if he had. But he said, "Not at all."

I took a step toward him, gesturing at the plant. My plant. "It's...very different, isn't it?"

"Lovely, I think," he said, but didn't look back at it.

I did. The little black label lettered in gold on the pedestal said *Pseudocolocasia Albaflora – Night's Crown.*

I had a horror it might be named something like Persephonia or Persephoneii. And it really was lovely, all black depths and star-white, a marriage of opposites. It was something my power had done that I could actually be proud of, even if no one knew but Gaia and me.

I returned my attention to my companion, apparently still politely waiting for me to respond or excuse myself. "I'm Perry," I said, extending a hand.

He just clasped his together and inclined his head. "Hadis."

He was so sad and grave I couldn't bear it.

"Come on, shake hands," I said with a laugh, reached out and took his hand.

There was a buzz of resistance then a jolt, like plunging your hand into a stream running straight out of a snowbank, cold so intense you can't tell if the water is steaming hot or icy.

My own magic gave a sort of lurching response, then it was just my hand in a man's warm one, or his in mine, though his was tense as though ready to be snatched away. His eyes (dark, I now saw, like the rest of him) were widened a little. Shock, I realized, and relaxed my fingers.

He, on the other hand, clasped tighter. "You," he breathed.

His voice held some strong emotion, and all I could think was, *Oh, man. I'm going to hear it now.* I hadn't meant to be pushy and obnoxious, but how else could he take it?

"The magic," he said, tipping his head toward the plant. "It's the same. This is your handiwork?" It was only just barely a question, more like he needed to be certain.

This was hardly what I expected, but I wasn't sure it was an improvement. "Well…yes. I…"

He released my hand and turned to the plant. As he had earlier, he reached out, but this time he did touch it, smoothing a finger along the edge of one velvety black leaf.

The leaf quivered under his hand. At first I thought it was responding to my upset, then I saw how his hand trembled. And I noticed next that the plant *wasn't* rustling, growing, shooting up dozens of flowers and generally acting like an ill-mannered dog on a chain. It just stood there quietly in its alcove, the way all plants had until recently.

"Remarkable," he said.

I, too, was thinking it was pretty remarkable, so it didn't occur to me to wonder what, exactly, he considered so remarkable. Or maybe if it did, I was thinking that he couldn't believe that someone my age could have produced such a paradigm of excellence in hybridization. Different genera and all that.

I wasn't getting a tongue-lashing, but I was nevertheless feeling more uncomfortable. He knew I'd ensorcelled this plant, which might lead to questions of under what circumstance said sorcery occurred, which would lead to all kinds of other questions I'd much prefer not to revisit: Zeusse, Aros, uncontrollable magic and the whole knotty, miserable mess.

I smiled. "Well, nice to meet you, Hadis." I offered my hand once more and this time, after the barest hesitation, he took it. "Enjoy the Plant Show."

He inclined his head again, and let me go.

I wove my way through plants and people, not paying much attention to either one. I wasn't sure what was going on in my head, either; I kept seeing Hadis' sadness and desperate restraint, feeling the icy cold of his magic in my right hand.

Why should he affect me like that? It had been nothing, just a glimpse of a private moment, the discomfort of the discovery of my inadvertent peeping. But what had been the emotion in his voice when he'd said, *You?*

I found myself at the hors d'oeuvre table. Fancy dishes arranged with flatbreads with rolled meats, crackers with spreads, delicate puffs on toothpicks covered the white tablecloth. A bowl of punch and little crystal cups stood at one end.

I stood staring at all of it like I was trying to decipher ancient hieroglyphics when a familiar voice said, "Looks like you've made a conquest."

I spun—no graceful and controlled turn for me. It was, naturally, Aros.

My heart started up like it had never slowed down, I wasn't quite sure whether from anger, anxiety or both. He wasn't the meltingly handsome young man he had been—now he looked sneering and mean.

I drew myself up and gave him my best impression of Mom's crop-withering glance. I never could do it as well as she can, but oh well. "What are you talking about?"

"Hadis," he said. "The Lord of Death himself."

I turned back to the food. "Go away, Aros. I don't want to talk to you."

"No wonder." His voice dripped with false enlightenment. "Since you prefer *that* type."

I rounded on him. I could not believe his gall.

"What type would *that* be, since we're talking about *types*?"

He grinned. The grin reminded me a lot of Zeusse at his nastiest and most vindictive. "Quite the necromancer, that one. You know, Perry—or maybe you don't, since your mother keeps you so secluded. A sorcerer who powers his magic with death." He leaned down. "You and I together would do much better, I promise," he whispered. His breath tickled my ear, my neck.

I stepped away. "Too bad all the evidence points to the contrary."

His cupid's-bow lips tightened, then he grinned again, a parody of that lopsided grin that had so engaged me. "Then to show you there're no hard feelings, I'll give you a little help. How's that?"

*No thanks*, I opened my mouth to say, but still grinning, he turned.

He held up two fingers to the waiter by the punch bowl. The waiter dipped out two cups of magenta liquid, each with a frozen raspberry bobbing on top.

Aros took both in one hand. Turning his back to the table in a furtive manner, he held my eye, raised a hand over one of the cups and made a little swirling motion. Magic sighed, releasing the heady scent of musk.

I scowled. I didn't know what he'd done, but he couldn't possibly expect me to drink that. "Aros—"

"Have fun, Perry," he said and wove away through the people around the tables, carrying the two glasses of punch.

"Aros!"

I started after him, but it seemed like every hole he slipped through closed up in front of me. It wasn't like I could elbow my way through this bunch of well-dressed strangers. I could just see punch splashed down shimmery dresses and tidbits on toothpicks smeared on expensive suits.

So I basically struggled along like a seal pup in choppy seas, straining to keep Aros' blond head in view. I lost him, but I had a bad feeling I'd better find him again. The quicker the better.

Finally breaking through the press in the middle of the room, I glanced frantically around. There he was, talking to— Hadis. Crap.

Aros was smiling and nodding with perfect ease. Hadis looked as grave as before, but didn't seem to mind the company.

Aros held only one cup of punch. I had a pretty good idea the other was the one in Hadis' hand.

*Okay*, I told myself, *don't panic. You don't even know what the spell is supposed to do.*

Plus Hadis had some heavy-duty magic going on—my hand *still* tingled. He'd notice any spell on that punch. See, he wasn't drinking. He was only holding it.

I nibbled a fingernail. My magic was no good for this kind of situation—it didn't do explosions or bursts of force or suddenly slippery cups. Maybe I should go rushing out and dash the cup from his hand. Sure, I'd make a complete fool of myself, but that wasn't the point.

But what if that *was* the point? Wouldn't Aros love it, both of us dripping with allegedly enchanted punch, bits of broken glass all over the floor that some hotel staffer would have to come and ostentatiously clean up.

Right! Of course! It couldn't be enchanted, because Hadis would know it, and would've thrown the stuff in Aros' face as quick as you could say, "You blackguard!" Or something like that.

On the other hand, did I really want to take the chance?

My dithering took place behind a rosebush with white blossoms blushing to violet. Women's voices had been gradually resolving themselves out of the general background noise, but I didn't dare look.

Then a familiar voice said, "Perry! I've been looking everywhere!"

Three women surrounded me, one of them Eleanor. I lost sight of Hadis for a second. When I spotted him again, *he was drinking*.

"Shit!" I hissed through my teeth.

"Bless you," one of the women said.

Eleanor peered at me. "Are you okay?"

What a question. Technically, the answer was "yes," but... That "but" mostly centered around what sort of mischief Aros was up to.

For Eleanor's benefit I said I was just fine, while glancing over at Aros and Hadis. Hadis wasn't clutching his throat or hunching over and growing lots of hair. He didn't seem to be behaving oddly (as if I knew him well enough to have any idea what odd would be).

Turning, Aros met my gaze and raised his glass. I couldn't tell if it was a mocking salute or if he was talking about me. Either way, Hadis turned, too. I instantly yanked my attention back to Eleanor and her friends, which was just as well because Eleanor was in the process of introducing everyone.

Really, what else could I do? Whatever chance I'd had at damage control was gone. Frankly, I was trying hard to convince myself that Aros had just been messing with my mind and there'd never been any need for damage control.

So I let them carry me back into the party, all of us gushing over the fantabulous plants. Although I wasn't doing it with a particularly easy mind, which irritated me because I knew I'd let Aros get one over on me.

I was still stewing over it when it was time for the formal presentation, and dammit! I was doing it again—letting Aros ruin the evening. I was going to sit down and enjoy this. I refused to think about him again. In fact, I only kept half my vow.

Eleanor sat beside me. The people filling the many other seats might have been opera-goers waiting for the house lights to go down—leaning heads together to converse quietly, rustling programs, stifling the occasional cough—except instead of sitting in plush theater seats, we were all perched on those tubular steel and industrial fabric chairs hotels provide for this kind of thing.

Finally, a plump, white-haired woman in a flowing, gauzy-looking dress of rich greens and browns stepped up to the podium and said, "Good evening, all. I am Gay Cosimia of TerraVisions."

I blinked, squinted, shook my head a little. She looked a lot like — no, just like — Gaia. As a matter of fact, she *was* Gaia. Here. At the Plant Show. At the Palace Suites in Modesto.

Questions came piling into my mind. One question, at least, was answered: why all these sorcerers were here.

I didn't keep track of much of what was said. Plants were rolled up on little draped tables and she talked about them. Then one, very familiar, was rolled forward, one with black leaves and white flowers.

I was glad I'd seen it before. If I hadn't, I would've jumped and gasped now, while I had an audience. This way I could just look properly amazed by its striking appearance.

Gaia turned one brown hand palm up in a graceful gesture, indicating the plant. "*Pseudocolocasia Albaflora* – Night's Crown, a very special creation made for a special person. Certainly, it is why my guest of honor is here with us tonight."

*Oh, gods*, I thought. *It's me.* She's going to call me up there with that same gesture, and then I...

Well, you know what happens when I'm under pressure.

Gaia said, "Please welcome...Hadis Aidoneu." She applauded, the audience applauded, Eleanor and I applauded.

A special creation made for...the guest of honor? But...

Eleanor leaned over and whispered, "Who the hell is he?"

I shook my head.

Straightening his tie, Hadis walked toward the front of the room slowly enough that I suspected he wanted to be there up about as much as I would have.

I held my breath and watched to see if he was twitching, or tugging at his collar (what did that spell do anyway?). He wasn't. But then, there wasn't any spell to begin with, was there?

Gaia held out both hands in welcome. Just as he reached her, he turned without taking her hands and faced the plant, facing the room in the process.

Gaia gracefully transformed the gesture into one of someone presenting something unique and amazing. People, that is, other sorcerers, in the audience muttered together as if Hadis' presence really were unique and amazing.

Behind me, a woman's voice whispered, "How can he be here? She must have him shielded. She's the only one who could."

Another woman whispered back, "Why? Who is he? I've never heard of him."

"I'm not surprised. I'll tell you later."

My ears perked up. What was going on? I'd sensed...something when I'd taken his hand. Had it been magical shielding? But why was it necessary for his presence? *Quite the necromancer, that one*, Aros had said, but that still didn't explain.

Hadis raised his hand to the plant, slid one long leaf between thumb and forefinger. He cleared his throat.

"I'm humbled and honored by such a gift." The mike picked up his voice, soft and grave and dark, spread it across the room. "You have outdone yourself, Gay. You have given me so much — so much more than I expected. Lovely."

As he spoke, his gaze swept the audience. I could've sworn it lingered in my general vicinity, then Gaia spoke her thanks and he turned to answer.

Eleanor leaned over and said, "That was strange. For a second there it seemed like he was staring at us."

"Yeah," I said, but those questions that had come tumbling down around me earlier were increasingly preoccupying. There were some real coincidences going on here, except that they didn't seem like coincidences at all.

That seemed to be the grand finale of the presentation. Gaia gave a few short closing words, then people around us started talking, getting to their feet, shuffling between the rows of chairs.

"Hey, listen," I said to Eleanor. "I want to try to

talk to her. You go ahead—it looks like I'll be waiting a while." I nodded at the inevitable crush converging on the presenter, in this case, Gaia.

Eleanor shot me a sideways glance, then shrugged. "Okay. I'll see you." She followed the crowd filtering its way back into the main room of the plant show.

I wasn't lying—it did take a while. At last, the courtiers thinned out sufficiently that Gaia saw me waiting.

"Perry." She held out her hands to me exactly as she had to Hadis.

The courtiers faded back like, *Whoa! She's on a first-name basis with this young person?*

I stood up from my chair, stepped forward and took her hands. *What's going on?* I wanted to blurt out, but I said, "The plants are wonderful. I love them."

"Ah," she said as if she knew what I hadn't said. "Please excuse us," she said to the last, clingiest audience members, all sorcerers.

Judging from the murmurs that had greeted Hadis, they probably had some questions of their own.

Gaia walked slowly toward the back of the room. Strange—she wasn't as short as I remembered her. But once the here-and-now becomes optional, I suppose a sorceress' physical manifestation can change at will.

But that was beside the point. What I really needed to be thinking about was how to broach the subject without sounding confrontational.

"You must feel yourself a victim of theft," she said, once more anticipating me.

"Oh, no," I said quickly. "I mean, the plant wasn't mine to begin with, just something I…" I flapped my hands. How could I keep from claiming ownership?

She smiled. "Something you made. And I have passed off your handiwork as my own."

There was that. I shrugged. "It would've been hard to explain to my friends how I managed to create a plant like that." Then another coincidence popped into my mind, because this seemed an event styled more for wholesalers and maybe an interested botanist or two. "Um… How many retail nursery owners received invitations to this show?"

"Oh, very few."

"Like, one?"

She only gave another of those Mona Lisa smiles.

Of course, there was no need to ask how she knew an invitation sent to Henry would ensure my attendance—don't forget, magic was involved. But I did have to ask, "Why?"

She turned to face me. "You were so troubled when I saw you last. I wished you to see the good your magic can do."

"Thank you. But… Well, it doesn't seem like that big a deal. Sure, I created something new…" I shrugged again.

We passed through the door into the main room of the Plant Show. Whether by design or accident, we pretty much had this end of the room to ourselves.

Gaia began walking again, hands clasped before her, the gauzy fabric of her dress whispering and flowing with each step. The colors seemed to change as I looked at it, the greens flowing through shades and hues, the browns increasing and diminishing. I'd gone river-rafting a couple of times on the Stanislaus, and the river was like that: the colors of the water deep and mellow or quick and bright, the banks sliding by with trees and vines and lawns.

"It is more than that," she said at last and glanced at me, a sharp, appraising look. She nodded. "Yes, I think you should know. You see, some time before you and I met, Hadis came to beg a boon of me, something he, for all his great power, could not have. I refused him that boon, but offered him another." She paused, then said, "It was you who granted it—a flower, living beauty, something he could cherish."

I shook my head. "I don't understand. You—" I was going to say surely she could have created something just as good, but that sounded arrogant.

She inclined her head. "I could have created it, yes. But I learned long ago to allow events to unfold as they will. You came disturbing me with your power. When I saw what that power could do, it seemed only proper that it should be allowed to fulfill the need brought to me."

I nodded. From an earth-sorceress standpoint, it made sense: let things grow according to their nature. Most systems tended to stay in equilibrium better that way, plus you didn't have to coddle them along to keep them healthy.

But I couldn't help wondering...what boon had Hadis asked for that Gaia had refused? And what, if he was so powerful, had made him seek the aid of another sorcerer — especially one as powerful as Gaia?

# III

Eleanor and I dutifully reported in to Henry on Monday. Eleanor, not having any personal dramas going on at the time, had kept better notes than I. She seemed to have memorized the names, breeding and landscape uses of all the plants we saw there. There wasn't much I could contribute.

"Did you even go?" Henry asked me.

Eleanor grinned. "She was busy breaking another heart, Henry. The guest of honor, no less. He had it bad, too — wherever Perry was, that's where he was looking."

Shock — or panic — shot through me. "*What?*" This was the first I'd heard of it.

She laughed. "Come on, Perry. I know you're not as naive as you pretend to be."

"I *swear* — "

"All right," Henry said, waving a hand. "Save the soap operas for girls' night out. Tell me about the plants."

And that was the last either of us (Eleanor and I, that is — Henry didn't care) talked about it.

Not, however, the last I thought about it, not to mention worrying about that spell Aros had put (or not put) on the punch. I hadn't told Mom what happened, mostly because she would have invited

Aros over for supper and then chopped him up in a stew and served him to Zeusse.

Okay, that's a bit of an exaggeration, but not much. Trust me.

Although in principle I didn't greatly object to such an event, I knew if Mom went off on a tear, no matter how well justified, I'd end up feeling guilty and responsible. I'd think I should have been mature and competent enough to deal with my own problems without running to mommy.

Anyway, I spent the next few weeks blithely thinking everything had gone back to normal, wildly growing vegetation, pantingly amorous couples and all. Aros was history. Zeusse didn't darken our doorstep, a curious happenstance given his earlier persistence. This should have warned me that all was not well and good.

There were other clues, if I'd only bothered to pay attention. The black horse I saw grazing a few times in the sugar beet field across the road from our house. The strange dead patches in the grass, like footprints. Sure, you didn't see very many horses grazing in sugar beet fields, but this *was* a rural area, and horses *are* known to reside in rural areas. The dead patches might've been webworms or cinch bugs; anyway, when I tutted over them, the grass happily grew back so it wasn't a big deal.

Such non-mysteries didn't enter the picture when one of those last-gasp heat waves rolled in around the middle of September, when it's ninety-something, the kids are running around in their back-to-school shorts and there isn't a yellow leaf in sight.

Eleanor and I were frantically watering for the third time that day. Thankfully, Henry didn't have a problem with short overalls, but both of us were still drippy. We didn't deign to squirt each other, but weren't above spraying ourselves with the hoses from time to time. It wasn't enough.

I had two words for the problem: "Tuolumne Reservoir."

Eleanor blew through her lips like a horse and nodded. "Straight after work."

"Done," I said.

Most of the reservoirs are on the east side of the Valley, in the Sierra foothills. Down come the rivers from the mountains only to meet dams on their way to the San Joaquin. The higher ones are usually flood control and hydroelectric projects, the lower for irrigation. The latter tend to make better swimming lakes since they aren't as cold and deep and there aren't usually as many maniacs in ski boats roaring around. Plus, even though they're a way from where we lived, they weren't as far as the big lakes higher up.

So we still had some afternoon left by the time Eleanor idled her truck down to a likely-looking spot by the shore.

It was a weekday, which meant we had the whole inlet to ourselves—nobody to stare at us for swimming in our work clothes. We'd done just that for a while and were leaning back on our elbows in the grass, watching the sun get all orange and blobby in the haze of Valley hydrocarbons, smoke and field dust, and feeling pretty content.

"Think we ought to head home?" Eleanor asked.

I tilted my head to one side, considering. "We've still got some daylight left. Let's walk around."

These weren't real hills here, but the land wasn't Valley-flat, either. We moseyed up a swell of land to see the lake stretching off coppery and crinkled in the late light, then dipped down again with a view only of the next rise, the liquid blue-green of the evening sky and a few black, spiky-looking trees. With the variation of water level, most of the trees were dead, but a few on higher ground owned a branch or two valiantly struggling along.

We were skirting a muddy patch, evidence of the lake's pre-irrigation release level, when Eleanor said, "Look at that."

I shaded my eyes against the slanting light. "What?"

"That." She pointed. "See? That black thing. Like that plant at the Plant Show."

I laughed, but sure enough, there was something black underneath one of the trees. "It's just another dead tree," I said. "A little one."

She shook her head. "No, it looks just like that plant. See the leaves?" She turned away from the shoreline and started tramping inland.

I followed her. "Come on, Eleanor. It's just a

weed, then. What would that plant be doing out here?"

She shrugged. "You're probably right. But it sure looks like it."

In our shorts and shoes without socks, both of us stepped carefully through the weeds, dead and scratchy at summer's end. The closer we came to the plant, damned if it didn't seem she was right. Then we were standing right next to it, staring in disbelief: *Pseudocolocacia Albaflora*, Night's Crown.

It didn't rustle or unfurl new shoots or buds as I watched. It just sat there, a fountain of leaves turned perfectly black by the low, reddish light.

Something felt *so* not right about this. I looked around.

So did Eleanor. "There's more."

The top of another black clump peeked up from behind a screen of weeds on higher ground. She marched up the little fold of land where we stood.

"Come on—we'd better check them out. If it's spread like this, it must be highly invasive."

Oh, gods. Leave it to me to create something that spread like the locust of weeds.

I started after her, dry weeds crunching under my feet. "You think they…escaped?"

"Well, I'd hazard a guess this area isn't part of a landscaping project."

I suppose this meant slinking to Gaia and telling her what was going on, something I definitely didn't look forward to. She'd wanted to show me the good my power could do, and now—

The world shifted a little, just a sort of slightly tipsy sway. *Gaia!* I thought for a second, because it felt a lot like that, when she'd opened the way between worlds to make her appearance. Then I realized it wasn't anything nearly so alarming.

Eleanor flung out a hand as if she'd lost her balance. "Hey, earthquake. Did you feel it?"

"Yeah," I said. "Just a little one."

For a true Californian, anything below a five on the Richter scale doesn't warrant more than passing notice. Really. You can always tell newcomers to the state because they get so worked up over earthquakes.

We were cupped in a sort of hollow between a couple of hills not much more than twice our height. The lake was behind us, out of sight. Twilight filled the place, seeming dimmer after the sunset glare on the water.

Both of us stopped, looking around. Fountains of dark leaves dotted the ground, here, here, where they had no business being. Somewhere behind us, a bird cried, a strange call I didn't recognize. Eleanor turned and started up the nearest hill. I took two steps after her—

The ground started jerking around. Above me, Eleanor screamed. I hit the ground on my side, jarring my elbow and shoulder. I'm not sure whether I screamed or not, but I felt like a lotto ball being shaken down into the chute, jiggled toward the lowest part of the hollow. Dust filled the air, and the smell of dust and old, crushed weeds, and another smell, one of broken roots, a smell as sharp as blood.

"Perry!" Eleanor screamed. "Oh my god, Perry!"

She lurched down the hill, eyes and mouth wide, hands stretched toward me. The world jumped like an old home movie off the sprocket. I scrabbled at the ground, trying to drag myself toward her, but it seemed to have gone soft—earth slipped under my paddling feet, oozed through my fingers like wet sand, except it was dry, crumbs and clods held together with a frail webwork of roots. Cold air suddenly breathed on me. I looked back—

*A black funnel gaped at the bottom of the hollow.* My feet hung over the very edge of it. The Night's Crowns ringing it thrashed and flailed at the mouth of the maw, the thing like a tornado sucking down into the earth, except there was no wind, no sound, nothing but Eleanor screaming, me screaming, kicking, clawing, the smell of deep, cold, dead places in my nose. One shoe fell off, fell in, and I was dangling.

Icy air fingered its way under my clothes. My hands clenched on a white, broken root. *Grow!* I willed it. *Grow!* It snaked off through the earth, burrowing, branching, grabbing new soil when the rest crumbled away.

Eleanor was there, on the perilous edge, sobbing in terror and scrabbling at my hands.

I think I was screaming, "Help me! Help me!"

Coffee-brown, wiry roots slithered out of the ground, wound around my wrists and forearms. Eleanor, with no way of knowing they were only answering me, gave a strangled cry of horror and started clawing at them.

"No!" I shrieked.

I shouldn't have bothered. The roots were already withering, turning dry, falling away as if blasted by fire. One of my hands clawed upward at nothing. The other held on to a single root. Eleanor's nails opened bleeding lines on my hands.

Feet braced wide on the edge above, she snatched uselessly at me as I fell.

You really don't expect anything in particular when you're dying—at least I didn't. If I had, I guess it would've been that horrible gut-swooping feeling of falling, maybe the terror of striking something, the crushing, smothering earth—yes, I'm an earth sorceress, but those whose magic works *inside* the earth are a whole 'nother breed from those of us who work with what grows out of it.

Which is to say I didn't expect to find myself surrounded by white light.

I know, I know. That's classic after-death experience, but I kind of thought you had to experience death first, and I hadn't. One second my last, tenuous grip was torn free and the next I was falling, floating, flying—it was impossible to say.

It was strange. I wasn't scared. In fact, I was perfectly comfortable, like when I was little and Mom would tuck me into bed at night, pull the blankets up to my chin and kiss me goodnight. My heart wasn't even jackhammering after everything that happened. I just drifted, for a second or an eternity.

The light began to shrink, a little darkness around the edges at first, then began to define itself as a thing, rather than an element. It became a vast globe like a sun seen up close, pulling away, away into the darkness, like a NASA simulation of a probe leaving the solar system. Smaller, dimmer, until it was like a full moon.

Gravity reasserted itself. I felt one direction as *down*, pressure against my feet. I wasn't ready for it and crumpled, landing sprawled on a cold surface.

"Perry," a voice said anxiously. "Are you well?"

*Well* echoed in my head. Well? Was I? I looked down at myself. I was scratched, filthy and missing a shoe. After everything, did that qualify as "well?" I looked up.

Hadis stood about arm's-length away, one hand outstretched as if to help me up, his face, his whole body tight as if in worry.

That globe of white light hung over his shoulder—more than one globe did. In fact, a whole line of them ran off into the distance, almost like streetlights, except the light was much softer, like moonlight. And streetlights have poles to hold them up whereas these had…nothing. Everything else was black—the walls, the floor, the scant furniture. It all gave the impression of a very austere foyer in a very large house.

I looked at Hadis again. Except for his obvious concern, he looked much the same as when I'd seen him last—carefully-combed hair, neatly-trimmed black beard and mustache—but he was dressed now in more informal dark shirt and slacks. He hadn't moved, but stood as if he were holding himself back. I must've been in shock, because I didn't feel much of anything, except really confused.

"I…um…" I levered myself up and his hand fell. I wobbled to my feet on my own and brushed at the dirt and mud all over me. "I…I think so. What happened?"

"Don't be frightened," he said. "You're quite safe." He folded his hands in front of him, seeming to fold up the worry or fear or whatever just as neatly.

My brain started working again, slowly. Hadis wasn't filthy and disheveled. And he hadn't answered my question.

"What happened?" I asked again. "Where am I?"

He looked around, as if seeing the place for the first time, like when you invite guests over and see all the cobwebs in the corners and spots on the carpet you missed.

"This is my home." Bitterness or resentment twisted his mouth, then it became composed again. "Welcome." Was that irony I heard in his voice?

"I don't understand." I probably sounded like an idiot, but I really didn't know what the hell was going on. Because obviously *something* was.

He took a step, gazing straight at me out of his dark eyes. They seemed even darker here under the light of the strange white globes. "I brought you here."

The words rang and rang in my head. "You—"

He was close, close enough I could touch him if only I raised my hand. His magic prickled my skin like snowflakes, delicate and cold, then an instant later, warm. I fell back a step, shaking my head. *I'm dreaming*, I told myself. It was too weird to be anything else. Hadis? Brought me here? But there'd been an earthquake...

He half-turned, indicating the way with a gesture. "Come."

I couldn't shake that horrible dissociated feeling, like I was a body going through the moves while *I* was somewhere else.

"I have to get back. Eleanor—" *Eleanor screaming, clawing at my hands.* I held them out: the bleeding lines were growing dark, scabbing over. She'd be in her truck by now, sobbing on her cell phone to Mom. "My mother will think something happened to me."

Hadis still held out his arm in invitation. "It can't be avoided. Please, come."

*Can't be avoided?* I wanted to bang my fists on my head: *wake up!* Or at least shake myself back into myself. What was wrong with me? Had I been that badly scared? Maybe I really had died. Hadn't Aros called Hadis the Lord of Death? But my hands were bleeding, my lungs and heart pumping.

I trailed along in the direction he indicated, half-shod, the stone floor icy on my bare foot.

Hadis fell into step beside me, walking as silently as...well, Death. My mismatched footsteps, however, echoed in high, dark places, whispering.

He gestured, and a pair of doors at least twice my height swung inward, also silently. As the light caught their surfaces, I saw a stern, bearded face carved on them, half of the face on each door. Walking through them felt like being swallowed.

The floor turned to marble, also black, inlaid with silver in strange, complex patterns. The magic in them tugged and nudged at me, but distantly, as if something lay between me and the magic. I had a feeling if Hadis hadn't been beside me, it would've carried me off...where? I glanced around. To one of those three other doors, all closed like corpse's mouths.

As it was, though, we were headed toward the door the magic wanted. It swung open and light spilled out.

If the white globes had been moons, this light was the sun's, brilliant and golden, although the air was still cold. The floor was green marble inlaid with some yellow metal—brass? Gold? I wasn't real up on my minerals. I blinked and perked up a little. A corridor stretched ahead, carpeted with a fancy Oriental runner and lined with more closed doors and tall, curtained alcoves.

I reached out and parted a heavy, brocaded

curtain as we walked by. A window lay behind it, of course. Then I saw it wasn't a real window, but only painted mullions with what looked like an English countryside with hills and trees and grazing sheep and a water meadow painted between. I snatched my hand back.

I think I would've bolted right then, but Hadis stopped, gestured a door open and said, "Here."

A smell of flowers wafted out. That was the only thing that held me, that kept me from spinning right out into the ozone, because believe you me, I think I was close to losing it.

I stepped past him into a pretty sitting room, all done in cream and lavender and green. A comfortable-looking upholstered chair with a footstool and a little side table sat before a hearth where a peachwood-scented fire burned. Two low bookshelves flanked the mantle. On the mantle, the table, the tops of the bookshelves, cut crystal bowls brimmed with dried lavender, rose petals, gardenia petals, the source of the flowery scent.

Hadis indicated an archway on the far side of the room. "Your bedroom is through there, and a bathroom, where you may wash."

I stood staring with my mouth open. I'm sure I looked a proper hillbilly with my dirty overalls and one bare foot and tangled hair straggling half out of its ponytail.

"Uh…thank you," I stammered. What was going through my head was, *wait, wait…* I took a breath. It shook, which didn't help my confidence. "But I have to go. Home."

He crossed to the door, resting one hand on the knob. His face was as expressionless as a judge's.

"I trust you will be comfortable. You must tell me if you need anything else."

He stepped through the door, and it closed gently behind him.

# IV

I just stood there, staring at the closed door. I didn't hear Hadis' footsteps outside in the corridor, only the voice of the fire, whispering. The scent of burning peach wood and lavender and gardenia and rose curled around me, a smell of remembered sunlight and summer air.

Leaning down to take off my other shoe, I still didn't feel anything at all. Then the terror I should've felt since that earthquake hit all at once. I crumpled to the floor where I lay curled on my side, in shock, I think.

I either passed out or fell into exhausted sleep, because I woke up on the floor staring into a diminished fire on the hearth.

The good news was I felt a little more myself; enough, at least, to get up and go investigate the bedroom. It was just as gorgeous as the sitting room without being overwhelming. The décor had lots of green with splashes of marigold-yellow and fuchsia and pansy-violet.

Going to sleep again was an appealing idea at the moment, but I dragged my filthy self into the bathroom, filled the Roman-style tub with hot water and lavender-and-vanilla-scented bath bubbles and climbed in.

I have to admit I was nervous about undressing,

but the bathroom door had a lock. Not that any lock would stop a sorcerer worthy of the designation, but it was a considerate gesture.

Wrapped in thick, forest-green towels, I explored the dressing room closet.

While I'd steeped in the hot tub and let the scent of lavender unravel my distraught nerves, I'd just about convinced myself that Hadis had somehow rescued me from that earthquake-opened pit.

Now, standing with the closet door open, seeing drawstring pants and jeans and comfortable cotton blouses, just the kind of thing I liked, I clenched the towel around me and backed up.

Okay, wait a minute, I told myself. This was probably more excellent hospitality. Like in fancy hotels where they provide robes for the guests. Maybe Hadis was just giving me a chance to spare Mom a fright before he returned me home.

Sure, and that required a complete wardrobe, right?

Staring at clothes and speculating wasn't going to get me any answers. I grabbed a pair of corduroys and an oxford shirt and put them on.

I had one bad moment at the door that had closed behind Hadis. I stared at the panels, chewing on a thumbnail, afraid to try the door. But the knob turned when I twisted it, the door opened, and the hall with the Oriental runner and brocade curtains covering the (nonexistent) windows appeared.

For a second, I thought it was empty, then I saw a

woman standing in the next curtain-alcove. Her head was turned as if she were gazing through the curtains and out the faux window.

"Excuse me," I said. "I'm looking for Hadis. Could you please point me in the right direction?"

She didn't answer but drifted toward me, her face still averted. At first I thought she was ignoring me, then I realized with a start she wasn't there. Which is to say, as an earth sorceress, I could tell that what stood with me in that hallway wasn't alive.

I looked at the softly flowing skirt, the face turned away and hidden behind a fall of hair and saw...a shade. An apparition. A ghost.

I came that close to jumping back into my room and slamming the door, but that would've been unspeakably rude. Plus she paused, as if to make sure I'd follow, then glided down the corridor to the left, the way I'd come with Hadis. This appeared helpful, so I followed.

Back we went through the door into the vast room with its magical traffic-control floor. This time I had the sense it wanted to push me back, but following my silent guide, I ignored it. The set of doors she led me to were, of course, black, but these were carved with a cross-eyed face with pointy teeth and a stuck-out tongue, like a Chinese or Indian demon.

The doors clanged, yawned open and we stepped (or I stepped—she drifted) into a vast, black hall.

Troughs of writhing flames lined a wide

causeway, casting a jerky red light. Perspective made it look as though they converged on a single, fiery point at the base of stairs as steep as those on a Mayan sacrificial temple. Magic and angles of silver inlay in the floor pointed inexorably forward, and forward I went behind my ghostly guide, toward the dark figure seated on a massive throne carved of obsidian at the top of those steps.

He stood—of course it was a he, with that height and those shoulders—and the bloody firelight played over a helmet crested with spikes, a voluminous black cloak, gauntlets and boots and leathers and steel. And then he said: "Perry." The voice boomed ominously inside the helmet.

I probably would've fallen on my face in abject terror, but he took off his helmet right about then.

Hadis' face appeared over a high collar. He set the helmet on the seat of the throne, strode down the steps like they weren't six inches deep and a foot high and came forward, cloak billowing out behind him. The flames lining the walkway died down until they were cheerful and rosy, like the fire in my room.

He turned to the shade. "Thank you, Lucy."

She nodded and floated back out. I stood there, eyeing Hadis' alarming outfit and fiddling with a button on my cuff.

It must've been pretty obvious, because he swept his hand downward and the Dark Lord getup disappeared. More ordinary slacks and shirt and jacket replaced it.

"Forgive me," he said. "I was working."

Doing what? I thought.

I was sure he'd started to offer his hand, but he ended up indicating the way back toward the dais. A couple of Queen Anne chairs now stood at the base, and we walked toward them.

"Lucy will be a companion to you," he said. "Are you comfortable with her?"

*Companion?* I opened my mouth to say, then changed my mind. I told myself it wouldn't be polite to start asking a bunch of impertinent questions. More like I was too unnerved to ask questions.

"Um…she's a little quiet, but just fine. Thanks."

He made a gesture, one I interpreted as regret. "The adage about the dead not speaking is quite true. You see, what made them…who they were has moved on, leaving behind only a shadow. A memory. Would you prefer I conjure something else? I fear…" He looked away. "Living company isn't possible here."

Part of me wondered, *Why not?* We sat down. I crossed my legs in a simulation of ease, but felt anything but easy. Even with the small, cheerful fires, this hall was forbidding. Not to mention the entire situation.

"Actually, since you'll be taking me home, I won't need a companion."

His black brows drew together. "You're unhappy here?"

"Don't get me wrong," I said quickly. "The room

is beautiful and I'm glad for the chance to rest and wash up. My mother would've freaked out if she'd seen me like I was, but if I don't show up soon to prove I'm still all in one piece, she'll really be upset, you know?"

He listened patiently to this speech then said, "Shall I send a simulacrum of you? I can create one that will convince her."

My stomach made a funny little dip. I folded my hands over my middle, hopefully to keep it still. "Um, no thanks. The genuine article will do."

He had a very direct, unsettling gaze. "Is your mother's concern your only objection to staying?"

Normally, I would've said, Hell, no! and proceeded to detail the manifold reasons I wanted to go home, now, please, preferably before I got here, thank you. In this particular case, however, I re-crossed my legs, groping frantically for a prudent reply.

"Your home is very grand and all, but... Well, I *am* an earth sorceress. And there's nothing alive here — or at least nothing I've seen so far."

Some dark emotion flashed in his eyes. "No," he said. "Nothing alive. Nothing but me — and you."

Hadis came to beg a boon of me, Gaia had said. A flower, living beauty, something he could cherish. *Oh, damn,* I thought. *Damn, damn...*

"So you see why I have to go back." I said it like of course he would.

"No, I don't." He stood, turned away. "What I

understand is that you don't *wish* to stay."

And here I was trying to be delicate. "Well…" I squirmed in my seat. "It's a little gloomy. For someone like me, you understand."

"You can be happy here," he said softly. "Tell me what else you wish. Anything."

I shook my head and opened my mouth to argue again, but he said, "Watch."

He raised a hand and the black throne room and the fires disappeared. I sat in a little white wrought iron chair with flowered cushions. Sunlight glanced through a towering confection of glass panes onto a cultivated jungle of tropical flowers. On either side of me, where the troughs of fire had been, water murmured down a series of stepped waterfalls. It was bright, beautiful, and entirely illusory.

"Hadis—"

"Wait."

The conservatory flicked into a large room with small curly sofas and chairs in white and gold damask. Musicians played chamber music and fancy-dressed men and women talked and laughed. I moved my hand and something flashed. A diamond (I somehow doubted it was CZ) the size of a pea perched on my finger—my ring finger. On my left hand. I started to my feet.

"Perhaps this is better?" he said.

The room turned into a barn with hay strewn on the floor and the fancy people into Mexican men and women. Mariachis played a lively tune, and the men swung the women in laughing circles. The diamond was still on my finger.

I squeezed my eyes closed. "Stop."

The mariachi music snapped off and the smell of hay wisped away, but I kept my eyes closed. My breath sounded loud and fast in the sudden silence.

"I can give you anything you wish, Perry," he said.

I searched my fingers with my left thumb. There was no ring. I opened my eyes, and the throne room was back.

Hadis stood behind his chair, gripping the back. "Anything," he said, "but send you away."

I looked away from the pleading and desperation on his face and sat down again. "Is it because of the plants?" I knew that wasn't it, but grabbed it and hung on. "The ones I made? We saw them at the lake, growing all over the place. I know I did something wrong—"

"Perry," he said. "You did nothing wrong. But the plants…"

I glanced up.

He drew a quick, swelling breath. "They showed me what is possible."

My throat closed. "What?" I whispered. "What's possible?" I was still pretending not to know.

He sat down again and leaned toward me. "You. Here. With me."

My eyes started aching like I was about to cry. *Okay, okay, stay calm*, I told myself. You know what's going on here. Tell him, so he knows too.

I swallowed, cleared my throat. "This isn't your fault." My voice wasn't entirely steady, but I continued, "It's a spell—"

"Spell?" He sat back.

"Yes, and the spell is because of me, because someone wanted to get back at me, so he…"

He watched me like I was about to unveil some lost and arcane knowledge.

"Well…he bewitched you. Aros did. When he gave you that punch." Now Hadis was going to ask how bewitching *him* got back at *me*, and I'd be in it worse than before.

He smiled. That was more alarming than the intent stare. "No sorcerer can bespell me. Not without my knowledge."

I knotted my hands together. "I didn't think it could work either, but… Hadis, you've kidnapped me. I know you couldn't help it. The spell and all. And if it wasn't for me, there wouldn't be a spell and you never would've done anything of the sort, because you don't seem like a carrying-off-the-damsel sort of guy to me. So when you send me home, I'll say it was all a mistake. I'll tell them there was an earthquake and you saved me, and everything will be fine."

He didn't seem about to say anything like, *I understand now, of course I'll send you home.* Getting a little desperate, I added, "Okay?"

Shaking his head, he said, "There is no mistake."

His hands were clasped between his knees. Unclasping them, he turned them palm up for a long moment, then slowly extended one. Cautiously, I put mine in his. I flinched. The sensation of his magic was like before—a shock of icy cold, then spreading warmth.

"Do you see?" he said, almost whispering. "You take my hand." He withdrew his again a little too quickly. "I touched the plant you made."

"But the spell—"

"The only magic belongs to you—all you can do, all you are."

"But…" My brain was like a car crash, bits flying everywhere. "I can't stay here." I shook my head. "I'll die." My voice came out very small.

"You will not die." He said it like a finality, a pronouncement of doom.

෫ඁ෪

I'd like to say I was plucky enough to go immediately to Plan B. I wasn't. I meekly accompanied Lucy back to my rooms. When I walked into my bedroom, something was different. Brighter. Then I saw what it was.

Sunlight angled across the bed from French doors that hadn't been there before. I dashed across the room, ran into the wash of brilliant, golden light and flung open the doors. Past a small porch, a dell full of green grass and arching white oaks stretched away. A woodpecker drilled somewhere in the distance. I smelled the musk of oak mast and the fragrance of grass.

And sensed not a single cell of life.

I don't know what happened, but I went off. Maybe I was sick of being scared and overwhelmed. Maybe I just plain didn't have the guts to go off on who I *should* have.

"Damn you!" I yelled. "Did you think you could trick me?" I slashed magic at the seductive illusion. It didn't even flicker. That made me even madder. I ripped off the oxford shirt, shoved off the corduroy pants and stood ranting in my bra and panties. "I don't want these. I want my *own* clothes. I want my *life!*"

I stormed into the bathroom, where I'd left my clothes. They weren't there. They weren't in the closet, either, or in any of the dresser drawers. I cursed steadily, using every foul word I knew in English and Spanish, but the only clothes I found were those Hadis had provided. I was not in a mood to be mollified.

I stood in the middle of the bedroom floor and shrieked, "What did you do with my goddamn clothes?"

Lucy appeared in the doorway holding a bundle. A green and white *dirty* bundle. Like a total bitch, I ran over and snatched it from her.

If it's possible to slam on clothes, that's what I did. They were stiff, muddy and lake-water-smelling, but I didn't care. I stalked out the French doors, across the porch and stomped through the grass. It felt like real grass, cool and slightly damp, the sun warm like real sunlight. I reached an oak and pounded on the trunk. It scraped my fist like real oak bark.

Yanking at the front of my filthy overalls, I shouted, "Look! This is real." Flakes of mud showered down. "Real dirt! Real *me!* Not like this…this bribery! If it was real, everything would be *growing like the world was about to end!*"

My voice cracked on that last bit, and I burst into tears. I sank down into the not-grass and pressed my face to my knees.

I didn't want to see an illusion so powerfully wrought it would've convinced almost anybody but an earth sorcerer. I didn't want to think about the sorcerer who was capable of creating something like this, who'd made up his mind that I was to be… No. I didn't want to think about that, either. So I just sat there, hugged my knees and sobbed until I thought I'd either throw up or pass out.

Eventually, I was reduced to gulps and sniffles, more from exhaustion than anything else. Wiping my nose and eyes, I raised my head. And started.

Lucy sat beside me in the grass, arms linked around knees, her skirt a spill of shimmery translucence in the grass. As always, her face was turned away as if she were gazing across the meadow. She didn't speak, didn't touch, didn't even look at me, but her presence was somehow comforting. Even if she wasn't alive.

"Lucy," I said.

Her head turned a little toward me, but not enough that I could see her face.

I felt totally drained, like I'd worked in a hot field all day. I just wanted to go back inside, crawl into bed and hide from everything. If I'd been completely alone, I might've done it. Trapped in this place where nothing grew, I might've slipped into the black waters of despair, stopped eating, stopped speaking, stopped moving. Turned into a — ghost.

I reached to touch her hand. I didn't meet flesh, but something else: a crackle of energy that resisted the pressure of my fingers, a sense of dense coldness.

According to Aros, Hadis was supposed to be a necromancer. "Is that what happened to you before you died?" I asked. "Did Hadis drag you here for his magic?"

I thought of his fingers trembling over the leaf of a Night's Crown. No. That was wrong — unfair. I couldn't imagine him hurting anything, much less any*one*. Maybe spirits, like Lucy, were what his magic drew power from. Besides, hadn't he promised I wouldn't die?

Lucy's head bowed slowly, as if from some sorrowful memory (did ghosts have memories?). Then she flowed upright.

I found myself on my feet too, as if she'd taken me by the hand and pulled me up. She moved toward the house, and I followed.

The French doors to my room were one of a series of doors on a four-story Mediterranean-style house. Mansion, actually. Since stucco and tile and wrought iron aren't alive, I couldn't tell for sure, but I suspected this was more impressively detailed illusion.

She drifted through the wrought iron railing. Since she had some physical presence and was capable of carrying things like, say, clothing, I had to wonder how this was accomplished. She did pause to open the door to the hallway, although this may just have been for my benefit. We turned right down the hallway, the opposite from the way I'd been before.

Of course the next question that came to mind was where she was taking me.

"Lucy, I hope you know I really don't have much of an urge to see Hadis right now, if that's where you're going."

She shook her head without pausing.

I hesitated at my door, then followed her. Walking through this…house, place, plane was much like walking through Gaia's. One minute we were walking along a hallway (with real windows now, through which not-real sunlight poured), and the next the hallway sort of petered out, like someone's interest or imagination had failed and stranded us in a jumble of rooms and ill-defined spaces.

The house illusion finally gave up the ghost, so to speak, and we were walking across the face of a dim, barren slope under a slate-colored sky. I shivered. I had a feeling this was the true nature of this plane, this chill, still deadness. The pop and crunch of small stones under my feet made the only sound.

How could Hadis bear to live in a place like this? Why would he even want to? More to the point, *what sort* of person would choose to live in such a place?

This cheerful thought sat on my shoulder all the way across one slope and up the face of another. I was irresistibly reminded of the slopes Eleanor and I had trooped up and down by the lake. And Lucy and I came to a little dell just like the one Eleanor and I had found. It, too, was filled…

With Night's Crown, all in brilliant white bloom.

I stopped. Lucy, beside me, pointed down. *More illusion*, I told myself, but I was already headed down that hill, because I knew it wasn't. That sunny, green dell with its oak trees and woodpecker had been fake. But this dim hollow under a blank, dreary sky held real living, growing things. On the awful, sterile-smelling air, I smelled a scent of citrus and honey and rainfall. I ran down the hill into the middle of the plants.

The way I felt while surrounded by those plants should've made them crowd around me like groupies. They just stood there so many diamond-studded crowns, too dignified for such vulgar behavior.

I touched their leaves, cool and velvety, stooped and probed the ground around their roots. It was real, moist earth in this place of bare, lifeless rock. Brought in, likely, then assiduously watered. It reminded me of a pretty bedroom and sunny French doors.

I stood up quickly, brushing leaves. Their rustling sounded just as loud in the silence as my footsteps. At least twenty Night's Crowns grew around me. All were blooming, new leaves furled like soft, black banners at the bases of the flower stalks.

But not a trace of the crazy growth other plants put on in my presence. Okay, granted, they weren't getting a lot of light and the gods knew the health of the beneficial bacteria in the soil here, but the plants at the lake and at the Plant Show hadn't grown wildly, either. I frowned. Yet they sure had at Gaia's. I'd propagated, sown and grown seedlings in the space of an hour. What was the difference between then and the other times?

I looked around. Here I was standing in a garden somewhere in the middle of this bleak plane of existence asking questions. A few minutes ago, I was ready to fold up and put myself away somewhere.

My magic needed living things. All alone, I'd probably self-destruct. With Hadis around to fill that gap, okay, I might not actually die (although as far as I was concerned, that was arguable), but I definitely needed more life in order to be myself.

I found a small plant, knelt and pushed my fingers into the soil around its roots. In a few minutes, I had a nice rootball on the ground beside me. Now all I needed was some burlap.

Lucy drifted toward me, sank down and held out

a fold of her skirt.

"Oh, Lucy," I said, because surrounded by glorious life, I'd forgotten all about what wasn't alive. And what wasn't alive had pulled me back from the edge of an abyss. I touched her hand again, that skin of static energy, that flesh of cold. "Thank you."

৪০০৪

The plant, growing in a bowl of Mexican pottery splashed with bright yellow and blue and orange, really helped my mental state. I wasn't reconciled to my situation by any means, but if I felt inclined to dissolve into tears or hide in bed with the covers pulled over my head, I had only to stroke the plant's leaves and the black feeling winding itself around my heart would dwindle.

Sitting on the floor in front of the French doors, I was doing just that. It was "afternoon" "outside." I didn't look at the "sun." It only enraged and scared me by turns, the first because it wasn't real, the second because an illusion that even behaved like the real thing was extremely impressive.

Let me put it this way. Except for Gaia, I didn't know of any sorcerer who could do such a thing, and I wasn't sure about even Gaia.

So anyway, I was in an uncertain frame of mind when someone knocked on the door. Since I didn't exactly expect a lot of visitors, I knew who it was.

I kept right on sitting on the floor, then thought, Well, okay. At least he's knocking. I got up and answered it.

Hadis, of course, stood outside. "Perry," he said. "Are you well? I haven't seen you …"

I opened my mouth to say, "What did you expect?" but he stepped quickly into the room.

Anybody else under any other circumstances, I would've said, "*Excuse* me?" But with *this* person under *these* circumstances, I stiffened in an instant of white panic, flinching away like I expected him to attack me. Ridiculous overreaction, I know, but I was still thinking of that damn spell of Aros'. And Hadis had, let's not mince words here, carried me off. What else might he do under the thrall of a spell cast by a sex magician?

But he only strode past me to the little Night's Crown perched on its stool in front of the French doors. I let out a breath.

He touched a white, ruffled petal, and I abruptly remembered the first time I'd seen him, at the plant show, his hand trembling over a leaf. This time his touch was gentle, almost loving. The shrinking reluctance was gone.

"You found them," he said.

"Lucy showed them to me."

He turned. "Lucy. Why?"

I wasn't too keen to admit I'd been on crying jags. On the other hand, guilt might serve to advance my cause.

I folded my arms. "I'm not the sort of creature that adapts well to captivity."

He twitched. "Captivity? You're free to go wherever you wish."

"Except—" I began angrily.

"Come. Let me show you this realm."

I didn't want to see his realm, especially not in the company of an irrationally enamored sorcerer. But he seemed calm and reasonable, and frankly, I wanted to make sure he stayed that way.

He opened the door for me and led the way to the left, pausing when he opened the door to the black hall with its four carved doors.

"I've encorcelled this room to…direct those who enter to certain doors. May I give you a token that will allow you to cross it freely?"

Strange grammatical construction, that *may I give you*. But I shrugged and said, "Sure."

He reached into the breast pocket of his shirt and produced…

Oh, dear. A ring.

I took it. It was gold with a blue stone, not too big, aquamarine or blue topaz. Or—ulp—blue diamond? I thought about testing it on an unobtrusive piece of glass somewhere. "Um…thanks."

So what was I supposed to do? Ask if he didn't have something more platonic, like a coin I could put in my pocket? He stood looking down at me while I held the ring and wondered if I should put *it* in my pocket.

I finally tried it on my right hand. Of course, it only fit the ring finger, but at least the right ring finger was better than the left. Although not by much.

I stepped onto the floor with its silver inlay. The magic flowed around me as if I were a rock and it a stream. I studied the doors: the one we'd just stepped through, the one through which I'd entered the first time, and the one with the demon-face, which led to Hadis' throne room. The fourth door bore a carving of an armored figure holding a bared sword.

So where did that one go?

Hadis swept a hand around the vast, echoing space. "You may go where you wish, but I would discourage you from visiting me in my workroom again."

Uh-huh. "Why?"

He remained silent for a few paces, then said, "My work is not always…pleasant."

I bet it wasn't. So then what, exactly, did a necromancer do? Raid morgues or slaughterhouses for working material? I swallowed. I couldn't think of anything more the opposite of what I did.

My lack of reply to this statement sounded loud as the echo of my footsteps. When we finally reached the door carved with the stern, bearded man, I was grateful when Hadis spoke.

"Did you know that rivers flow here?"

"No. What I saw was…dry."

"Life can't exist without water," he chided.

I'm not sure why, but this irritated me. "You said nothing lived here. Except you."

"And you," he added.

I refrained from pointing out that I did not *live* here, I was a prisoner.

"What about the plants?" I said. "The Night's Crown. Why didn't you tell me about those?"

Again that silence. I studied the white globes of light hanging like so many moons in the air.

Strange. So much of this place struck me as a stage set to shock and awe visitors. But according to Hadis, there were no visitors. No, wait. He'd only said no one *lived* here, because he'd just talked about the floor directing "those who enter." So who visited? More to the point, how did they leave again?

When he finally answered my question, I'd almost forgotten what I'd asked.

"It might have appeared that I was...collecting things of yours. I didn't wish—" He darted a glance at me. "I didn't wish to frighten you."

*Then why the hell did you drag me here to begin with?* Once more, I bit my tongue. If only he weren't so grave and gentle and concerned about my feelings. No, I take that back.

So it ended up being another of those uncomfortably silent moments. The white globe-moons fell behind. The light didn't diminish, but gradually turned ruddy. The temperature was going up, and the air had an acrid tinge, too, something I instinctively knew to be hostile to me and what I did.

I faltered. "What's that?"

"The River of Fire," he answered. "Don't be afraid."

"I'm not afraid. But you said water." I was getting *way* too many surprises here.

"Of course," he said quickly. "You don't care to see this?" This wasn't said plaintively, but in a tone of perfect politeness.

It made me feel like a whiney kid. "It's just that my magic is screaming to get the heck away from here. And I can't breathe."

Realization showed on his face. "Forgive me."

He gestured and the poisonous sense vanished. I might've been strolling along the seashore, surrounded by the tang of salt air. I drew a breath as if I'd been holding it too long.

"Better?" he asked.

I took another breath. "Yes. Much." Then added, "Thanks."

Craggy rocks rose all around, with a sheer face looming up to the right. The River of Fire was beautiful, in an awe-inspiring sort of way. A firefall of lava spilled down the cliff with a dull, low-frequency seethe, then crawled across the heaved and rumpled terrain. Heat waves shimmered like transparent veils.

I could see why my magic had reacted like it had: this was definitely not a habitable ecosystem. I was pretty sure even pyrophilic — heat-loving — bacteria wouldn't make it here.

We turned to the left. The River of Fire wound off somewhere into the distance — distance, I was learning, being a relative thing here. Or maybe Hadis was just moving us around by magic while we only seemed to be walking in the normal fashion.

Anyway, the land changed a lot more than I'd expect from twenty minutes or so of walking, becoming flatter, gentler, although not in the character of any land I knew. My instincts told me this should've been a much greener place than California. Certainly the river we came to was larger. In California, we're used to rivers you can throw a stone across if you have a good arm, not something whose far bank was veiled in mist.

Or was it mist? It seemed to be moving around an awful lot.

"The River of Woe," Hadis said.

I walked down to the bank. Grass and tulies and cattails should've grown here. Willows. Blackberries. I knelt and peered into water that should've combed the green hair of water weeds. I saw only clear water flowing over stones.

"Woe," I echoed. "Yes."

Sitting back on my haunches, I closed my eyes on the dead river. Then I thought, *For the gods' sake, Perry, you're a* sorceress. *This man is under a* spell. *Rather than feeling all put-upon, why don't you try to* remove *it?*

Okay, my magic made things grow. What did I want to grow? How about free will? Rational sense. Hmmm. Some empathy, maybe. Now the question was, would my power work on any of those? I gave it a pat on the head and slipped its leash to let it get its muddy pawprints all over Aros' spell.

"Perry," Hadis said. "What are you doing?"

Oops. "Oh, um, I…" Sighing, I stood and turned to face him. "To be perfectly honest, I'm trying to disenchant you."

One sharp, black brow rose. "In the literal sense, I see."

I shifted from one foot to the other. "Well…yes."

With the slightest quirk to the corner of his lips, he nodded thoughtfully. "But as I quite easily noticed your attempt, doesn't it follow that I'd notice the casting of the original spell?"

"Okay, you're right, I can't explain that part," I said, throwing up my hands. "But…well…what about what you've done, bringing me here? Wouldn't it have made a lot more sense to, say, go on a couple of dates first? Let me introduce you to my mom? You know, kind of start out slow and see where things go."

The little amused quirk on his lips disappeared. "That isn't possible."

"But…why not?"

He didn't answer.

My insides twisted like a wrung dishrag. "At least let me tell my mom I'm okay."

He turned away. "Perry—"

"Why not?" I insisted. "What can she do to you? You're the most powerful sorcerer I've ever seen."

He was gazing away across the landscape, but he turned to look at me then. I suddenly wished he hadn't.

"Yes," he gritted out. "I am the most powerful

sorcerer you will ever see."

He turned on his heel and stalked off. I didn't dare follow until he'd gotten some distance ahead.

# V

I have to admit, after our little spat, I really expected Hadis to wait for me at some point. He didn't. I went from feeling mystified and alarmed to mad.

*I'm the most powerful sorcerer you'll ever see.* So what was that supposed to mean? That he was so powerful he could do whatever he damn well pleased? How dare he get angry with me! *I* was the one held against my will in this horrible, barren place.

Not wanting to get lost in this nowhereland in any case, I kept him in sight until the anteroom with the white globes. I waited until he disappeared through the door at the far end, then waited a while longer, giving him time to get across the black hall.

By the time I got back to my room and I'd gone over our interchange for about the twenty-fifth time, I was beginning to think that he hadn't seemed angry and arrogant so much as in agony. The look on his face, full of loathing, the pain in his voice… What was with that?

I paced back and forth in front of the French doors, stewing. I didn't care what Hadis' problem was. What I cared about was getting out of here.

So how did I know that only really powerful sorcerers could open the ways between dimensions? Hell, who was to say *I* wasn't a really powerful sorcerer, and only needed the motivation to prove it? My magic certainly had enough horsepower to jerk me around like a semi tractor pulling a Volkswagen.

I picked up the little Night's Crown and carried it into the illusory meadow. Sure, nothing out there was real, but the simulation of sunlight and breeze and life, as long as I pretended it wasn't a simulation, gave me courage. The real plant gave my magic something to work off of.

Half an hour later—or an hour, or four, or whatever—the only thing I'd managed to accomplish was to give myself a headache. Or I suppose the headache might just possibly have had something to do with the fact that I hadn't eaten in something like 24 hours.

I pushed myself up, picked up the plant and plodded back inside.

Lucy hovered by the fireplace, the cheery flames flickering palely through her skirt. She gestured at a small table. A couple of covered dishes and a steaming cup sat on it, as well as a cut crystal vase with an arrangement of dried rosebuds and baby's breath. A little square of paper nestled among the flowers.

I folded my arms. "Uh-uh. Forget it. You can tell Hadis I'm on a hunger strike and I am *not* eating a single bite until I go home."

She lifted the cover off one of the dishes. Scrambled eggs, sausage, a toasted English muffin and a little crock of marmalade. My stomach rumbled like a cement mixer.

"Well…okay," I said. "Maybe just this once."

I sat down at the little table and dug in. Lucy sat in the chair opposite. I got the feeling she was watching me, even though, as usual, her face was turned away.

"Um, muffin?" I offered.

She shook her head.

"Tea?"

She shook her head again.

I looked at the items on the table and sighed. "The note, right?"

She nodded.

"Okay, I'll read it." I extracted the paper, showering fragile dried baby's breath, and unfolded it.

*Persephonie*, it read in a heavy, backslanted hand. Ooh, I thought. Using the long form, are we? I read on. *I beg you to forgive my behavior. I have no excuse for burdening you with troubles which have nothing to do with you. My feelings are quite the contrary, I assure you. I promise it will never happen again.*

"Right." I answered aloud. "But I don't hear you telling me what a terrible mistake you've made and how you'll send me home right after breakfast."

*Hello*, Perry. Did I really intend to wait around for Hadis to see the error of his ways? Okay, fine. Aros' spell was more than my magic or knowledge could deal with. Same with opening a way back to the real world. But there was one door in the black hall I hadn't been through yet, the one all the magic pushed away from. If I wasn't going to check it out before I gave up, I deserved my captivity.

I forced the bite past the knot in my throat and finished the rest of my breakfast.

Lucy came with me when I got up and headed for the black hall. When I reached the door with the armored, sword-bearing figure, though, she peeled off like she'd suddenly remembered an important appointment elsewhere.

This was not encouraging. Nevertheless, I wet my lips, shook back my hair and pushed open the door.

It would've been nice to find a big, green "EXIT" sign with an arrow. Yeah, I know. Dream on.

Instead, I stepped into what looked like the entry foyer to an M.C. Escher drawing, complete with a confusing array of doors, staircases and galleries. In the middle of the black-and-white tiled floor lay what looked like a huge heap of fur someone had carelessly dropped.

Except this heap of fur had a paw about the diameter of my own leg sticking out from it, and the paw had four black toenails the size of large pea pods.

Needless to say, I came to an abrupt stop. The fur heap raised its head. This was a definite loophole to Hadis' promise of "you may go anywhere you wish."

The "this" in question was a dog. An extremely large dog, one that looked like a cross between a Rottweiler and a bull mastiff. The head was probably twice the size of my own, and it looked at me out of its round, brown eyes. It stuck out another paw and raised —

Two more heads.

Now if I'd been tempted to think I'd stumbled on another living creature, the second and third head would've instantly set me straight. Nevertheless, I scrambled backward.

I know. Never run from a dog—it triggers their predatory instincts. But the sight of an enormous, three-headed dog triggered *my* flight instinct, and I wasn't thinking of much else.

It raised its hindquarters and stretched. All three heads yawned, curling pink tongues between very white teeth.

"Well," it said. "It's the little sorceress. Hello."

I stopped again and stood there quivering. "H-hi," I squeaked.

It blinked three pairs of eyes. "Ah. I'm being discourteous. I am Cerberus."

When it spoke, all three heads talked, so it was more like, "I am Cer—" "—ber—" "-us." Along with the quality of diction, it was very disconcerting.

"Oh," I said, and stared at it—him—until I remembered you're not supposed to stare dogs in the eye—eyes. It's interpreted as aggression. I looked down at those paws the size of dinner plates. "I—um—I'm Perry."

"Honored to meet you, Perry." The paws stretched out and the toes flexed as he lay down again. "The master told me to expect you."

"He did?"

"Oh, yes. I was delighted when he said he'd brought—" Here two of the heads turned, snapping and snarling, at the third. It ducked, stretching its lips in a submissive grin. "Excuse me," the other two heads continued. "As I was saying, I was delighted when he told me about you."

The other head moped on one paw. I wondered what it had been about to say. "You were? Why?"

"Well," the third head began cautiously. "The master is so very lonely, you see," the other two heads went on. "There are times I've feared greatly for his wellbeing. I speak with him and bear him company from time to time, but he needs his own kind."

This sounded like one of those situations in which people set themselves up for their own misery. "Then why does he hang around here? This plane isn't exactly a social hot spot."

"I have often asked myself the same thing. However, all I can tell you is that the master rarely leaves this place."

It was weird to be standing in the foyer of this Winchester Mystery House on steroids, talking to a dog who sounded like he'd attended an Ivy League college, but at least I was finally getting some answers.

I folded my arms. "So who made me the official keeper of company? I'm sure there are millions of other people more interesting and far better suited than I am."

The three heads shook emphatically. "Not at all. You're perfectly suited."

"*Excuse* me," I said, "but I'm an earth sorceress. I've only been here a day and I'm already getting ragged around the edges."

"Precisely the point." His tail wagged. "You've been here a day, and you, of all creation, are only a bit strained."

One of us was definitely not getting it here.

"Okay, I'll tell you what," I said. "Someone can point me to the way out. I'll go to the nursery where I work, use my employee discount to get one of everything and bring it all here. Do you think your master might see his way clear to letting me go then?"

Of course, it would've made a lot more sense to put this proposition to Hadis, but after yesterday, I was a little wary about piping up with any more good ideas.

"I fear you misunderstand, Perry."

I threw up my hands. "What is there to misunderstand? I've been dragged to this terrible place where the sun doesn't shine, the wind doesn't blow, nothing grows, nothing breathes, nothing *lives* —" My voice was getting higher and higher. I stopped and swallowed hard.

"It isn't simply a matter that nothing lives here," Cerberus said gently. "It is that nothing *can*. Nothing but you."

I stared at him. Gaia had said, *I offered him a flower,*

*living beauty, something he could cherish.* And Hadis had said, amazed, *You took my hand.* A suspicion began to take shape in my mind, something I couldn't quite put my finger on, but that made me go cold all over. Or maybe it was more than a suspicion, but I couldn't bear to face it. It, and its implications.

I said, "I don't understand."

He sighed. "Neither do I." He pronounced it *nye-ther*. "I am merely a conjuration, and so cannot sense the pulse of life as can you and the master. I know only that the first gleam of hope I've yet seen in him came with you. For that I am grateful, and shall endeavor to serve you as faithfully as I serve him." And this fearful apparition lolled out its three tongues and flattened its six ears in a dog's smile.

This glimpse of a despairing Hadis caught me. He'd seemed so...so powerful, so self-contained—

Cerberus said, "The master said to allow you to go where you will. "That," his leftmost head nodded to my right, to a series of red doors and a staircase carpeted in black and white, "is where the specters stay. They're unable to harm you, but they can still frighten."

"Lucy—the, um, girl who keeps me company— doesn't have to stay there, does she?"

No wonder she'd made tracks in the other direction if she'd once been stuck in the middle of frightening shades.

The righthand head glanced back. "The master brought her through there after you came."

I peered past his right shoulder at a solitary door that looked like it must lead to a dungeon, all blackened wood and iron bindings. "Where does that one go?"

"I know only that the master spends much time within."

Ooh. Now that was interesting. "Is Hadis in there now?"

"No, not now."

"I guess that's where I'm going, then. Thanks for your help."

"I am always at your service," he said, stepping aside.

The inner door, too, opened easily under my hand, though it sighed as the one that opened onto the black hall hadn't.

Please, please, I thought, let this be the way out...

I stepped into a room, a very ordinary, middle-class room with wall-to-wall shag carpet, a couch and chairs, a coffee table with books and magazines scattered across it, and an old console TV in the corner. A picture window looked out onto a quiet residential street, sidewalks, a lawn drifted with fall leaves. Through another door to my left came voices.

"*Yesss!*" I whispered. All I'd had to do was stick with it, find the right door, and bam, I was back in the real world. *Where* in the real world was another question, but I'd worry about that later.

I bit my lip. Well, here goes. If they called the cops, at least I'd get a free phone call.

I knocked firmly on the front door as if I'd found it open. "Hello-o-o!" I called. "Anybody home?"

The confused, happy babble continued in the other room.

"Excuse me," I went on. "I don't mean to barge in, but I wonder if I could use your phone."

I made my way toward the voices, the banter of children, a woman's rich laugh, a man's deep, good-humored tones.

A man, a woman, and four kids wearing silly pointed birthday hats sat around a table littered with plates and half a birthday cake with a big "13" on it. None of them even glanced at the intruder—me, that is—standing in the doorway of their dining room. How weird.

Two of the younger children dueled with those paper party favors that toot and uncurl when you blow in them. A young girl sitting in the middle of a pile of birthday present debris held a new sweater to her chest and mugged for an older boy with a camera pressed to his face. The woman—the mother, obviously—sat leaning into her husband, smiling. She was beautiful in a powerful sort of way, with thick brows, full lips and a strong chin.

The flash popped, dazzling my eyes. When I'd finally blinked the spots away, the boy had put down his camera and was shooting his party trumpet at his sister's nose.

Black hair. Dark eyes. For a second I thought he must be Hadis' kid brother or son. Then I caught my breath.

"*Hadis?*" I said.

Don't ask me how I knew—I just did. This was a very young Hadis, a Hadis who couldn't yet grow a beard and mustache. He was laughing, ducking the uncurling ribbon of paper his sister blew at him. Which meant...

I sagged against the door frame. This wasn't the real world. It was the past.

No one paid the least attention to me. I might've been the ghost, drifting unseen and unheard around the edges of this happy family gathering.

I circled the table, watching. The father had Hadis' dark good looks (or Hadis had his, I suppose), but was craggier, more angular, more elemental somehow.

The younger boy knocked over a glass of milk in the heat of birthday-trumpet battle. The father gestured, and the spill spreading across the table stopped and ran *back* toward the glass. The white wave piled in and the glass tipped itself upright.

Wow. I'd never seen sorcery like that before.

Young Hadis watched just as eagerly. "When will I be able to do that, Dad?"

His father laughed. "When it's time. Just be patient."

"But you could *make* it time," Hadis persisted.

*He could?* I thought.

"I could," the father said, "but I won't. You have to wait like everyone else."

The woman raised a teasing brow. "Don't you want to be able to do what I do?"

Hadis flushed. "That's girl stuff!"

"Tell that to all the doctors who deliver babies," she said with a wry smile.

The father ran a finger through her rich brown hair and murmured, "Not all of it is girl stuff."

His mouth was close to her ear, and his breath must be tickling it. She turned and kissed him, a good, hard buss not inappropriate in front of the kids, but also one that promised a lot more later.

I turned and scurried out through another door. The sight of that face so much like Hadis' kept running through my head, the teasing laughter in his voice, the caress of his fingers through his wife's hair.

Heat went through me, and it wasn't entirely a blush. *Oh, come* on, *Perry*, I told myself. *It's not like this is the first time you've seen people kiss!* So why was I all hot and bothered now? Why was I running away like...like I was being chased by a giant three-headed dog?

୫୦ଓଃ

I had three strikes against me. Unfortunately, I was *not* out. That left figuring out what kept Hadis here if he was "so very lonely," and why I got so lucky as to be the chosen companion of his exile.

I know. It all sounds so Beauty-and-the-Beastish, but at least a mystery gave me something to think about besides the fact that I was pinned like a butterfly. Maybe I couldn't magic my way out, but I could still try to puzzle my way free. And if I stumbled across something within these memories that might give me some leverage over Hadis, so much the better.

Because obviously, that's what these were: Hadis' memories. Some were bright and clear as if etched in crystal. Others were fuzzy and silent, like those old eight-millimeter home movies where black-and-white people in funny clothes and hairdos wave and mouth at the camera.

I explored his bedroom, filled with model airplanes and posters of aircraft from barnstormers to the Blue Angels. I leaned my elbows on his windowsill and watched him set off model rockets in the backyard.

I discovered he had a penchant for creatures: an oscar fish swam in a small aquarium on a shelf, a fuzzy caterpillar munched leaves in a jar with holes punched in the lid, gerbils ran in an exercise wheel their cage, a lizard pounced on crickets in a terrarium decorated with smooth stones, a branch and a small dish of water. The finches that chattered in the family room were ostensibly his sister's, but Hadis was the one who fed them and changed the papers on the bottom of the cage. And the family dog, a big, ugly, familiar-looking mutt that looked like a cross between a Rottweiler and a bull mastiff, followed him everywhere, except when he shot off the rockets.

So where was the disconnect between the kid on

the school debate team, the one whose good looks made him so popular with the girls while not alienating the guys, and the grim, intense sorcerer I knew? Something to do with his magic?

The strange thing was, I saw no sign of it. A sorcerer's powers usually manifest a year or two after puberty. Like I said, mine came on really late.

I saw Hadis with a humongous crush on a girl called Menthie in junior high. I watched him try to wheedle his dad into letting him take the car to a friend's party, and agonize over his SAT's. But no magic.

I was searching for a way to escape, so it makes sense that I began to get pretty single-minded in pursuing my means to that end. Okay, I'll admit it: maybe even a little obsessed with those means. I mean, under the circumstances, it's not unreasonable. Right?

I spent my days with memories of Hadis as a little kid, as a boy, a young guy with his quick grin and wicked sense of humor. Kind of like reading a story you just can't put down. Even when you aren't actually reading it, it possesses you, fills your imagination, makes you wish you could leave the everyday world and live in the story's world.

This went on for...I don't know how long. I'd guess a week or so, but it might've been longer. I lost track after a while.

Anyway, one day I happened upon a Yule scene. The family was gathered in the living room in their robes and slippers opening presents.

Which made the stranger standing with his back to me all the more conspicuous, because he was wearing a long coat. He wasn't opening any presents, either, just watching. I came closer, curious, and he turned.

"Hadis," I blurted. This was the present Hadis, the one I knew, the sorcerer with the beard and mustache, not the kid hanging over the radio-controlled P-40E Flying Tiger he'd just unwrapped.

"I—I'm sorry," I said. Gods. I was mortally embarrassed. *Now* I felt like a peeping Tom. I turned to leave—to flee, more like.

"Wait," he said. "You don't need to go."

"But—I—oh..." I stood there with not a clue what to say.

He took a step toward me. Behind him, the family continued unwrapping presents. "Cerberus didn't explain you're welcome here?"

"Yes—yes, he did..." I fumbled for something else to say. "Thanks."

In the memory, the younger sister squealed, "An Easy-Bake Oven!"

Hadis turned to the scene and smiled. "That was one of my favorite Yuletides. I'd been sick with the flu for a week, notwithstanding all Mother could do. After I unwrapped that plane, I mended with a vengeance."

I realized with a start it was the first time I'd seen him smile like that, with tenderness. His present-self, that is. I turned quickly, flustered, though I couldn't have said why. The mother, lifting a frothy bit of lace and not much else from silver tissue paper, exclaimed in delight.

"I like your parents," I said, somewhat at random. I felt so awkward. "They seem really nice."

He nodded slowly, but the smile died. "They were."

*Were?* "Your brother and sisters," I went on desperately. "Are they sorcerers, too?"

"No," he said. Politely, yet quite decisively.

I shut up. I was *not* doing well here. "Hadis…" I ventured.

The dark look on his face lightened a little.

I took this as encouragement. "I don't mean to make you mad. Honestly, I'm not trying to."

He took my hands. "No, Perry. In no way am I angry with you."

I stared at my hands clasped against his heart and thought of the times I'd seen his father hold his mother's hands like that, bending his dark head to kiss her fingers…

I must've stirred because he relaxed his grasp, letting me slide free.

"I enjoy visiting here," he said. "I find it…settles my mind."

So what made it *un*settled? "I like it, too," I said instead. I debated a second, decided it was safe and said, "Your family —" I stumbled there, almost saying *is*. "–was a lot different from mine. There's only ever been Mom and me, and we hardly ever lived in a town."

"Weren't you lonely?"

I shrugged. "No. Rural communities are very close. Everybody knows everybody. Plus Mom is always busy, and I'd go everywhere with her…" I sighed and fell silent.

"You miss her," Hadis said.

I nodded, chastened. His mother was dead. These shades were all he'd ever see of her again.

"I understand." He looked away and murmured, "It is, after all, very lonely here."

A servo whirred, tilting ailerons as Hadis-the-boy worked the controller. "Wow! Neat! It's gonna fly just like a real plane!"

I looked back to Hadis' half-averted face as he watched his younger self. *Then why do you stay?* I opened my mouth to say, but he spoke first.

"At that age, I wanted to be a pilot or an astronaut, then a veterinarian when I was older. Mother was pleased with the idea of my becoming a healer—" His lips closed in a line of pain.

He glanced at me and seemed to collect himself. "I know you're uncomfortable with illusions, but you seem to find amusement in these memories, even as I do. Have you ever flown?"

Now with a sorcerer, that can be a very literal question, but whether by magic or in the usual way, the answer was "no." I shook my head.

He extended a hand. "Then come."

I put my hand in his, and he encircled my fingers in a warm grasp.

We stepped through a door into a summertime woods. The glimmer of a lake was visible between the trunks, and a smell of wood smoke drifted on the air. A child's voice echoed under the trees. We ducked under low branches and came out onto the bright, windy field of another memory.

Puffy clouds dotted a sky the blue of the stone in the ring Hadis had given me. Brown, prickly weeds bordered strips of asphalt, and rows of hangars and a squat tower crouched to one side. Not far away a couple of guys were dragging a cable attached to a small plane toward another plane, low and silver with long, thin wings like an albatross'. They hooked it under the nose of the smaller plane, then the plane in front rolled forward a little, taking up the slack.

"Come on!" Hadis said and ran for the towed plane.

"But—!"

For a second I glimpsed an image of a young Hadis and his father in the seats. They flickered away, then the present-day Hadis clambered into the cockpit, hauling me into the forward seat. The canopy shut.

"But," I said again, "how can we be in the memory?"

"Can't you take part in your own memories?"

He had a point. Where I came in was another question.

The plane in front blatted suddenly, its propellers blurring first clockwise, then counterclockwise, then we were heading down runway, faster, faster. A weird stomach-dipping lurch came and all the bumps and vibrations of the pavement ceased. I peered out the canopy.

I'm happy to say I didn't panic when the ground dropped away, tilting at an angle that sent my inner ear scrambling. The runway and taxiways turned into straight-ruled lines. A freeway appeared, cars and trucks beetling along it, winking in the sun, then a town, then a landscape like a topo map dotted with brown and green. There was a *bang*, a jerk, and world and sky wheeled with a quiet rush of air.

I didn't quite scream, but maybe I squeaked a little. Behind me, Hadis whooped with joy. A sudden urge to see that joy grabbed me, and I sneaked a look back over my shoulder.

I saw instead a hard glitter of white teeth in the black beard, as if he defied something even more powerful than himself. Something that would crush him if it could.

I snatched my gaze forward again, to the circle of earth and sky beyond the scratched Plexiglas of the canopy.

That was ridiculous, I thought. What could be stronger than he was? He'd said himself he was the most powerful sorcerer I'd ever see.

*Yeah*, part of my mind whispered. Then why did Cerberus say he feared for "the master's" wellbeing?

Why did Hadis stay here *all alone?*

"I revel in this freedom," he said. "The sun, the wind, all the world spread out below."

Freedom. Sun, wind. He craved it too?

"Are you enjoying it, Perry?"

"I—yes. Very much." Even though it was only one step removed from illusion, I felt...different. Almost like I shared an adventure with...a friend.

Like a *what* with *what?*

"It will be coming to an end soon, though," he said. "It was only a half-hour flight."

The glider sailed down, down again, leaving the open sky with its popcorn-puffy clouds for reality.

My mood went down with it. The Hadis who helped me out of the glider once on the ground was the reserved, serious one I knew. But a remembered glint of sunlight gleamed in his dark eyes.

"It was good..." he said and paused. "...to share that with someone."

I nodded, staring at the weeds verging the runway. The wind rattled them, and they prickled through my socks.

Why did I feel so glum? I'd learned something today, hadn't I? If only I could get myself to puzzle over how I could use it.

He walked beside me in silence for a while, then said, "Will you accompany me again?"

Just like that, the glumness was gone. "I'd—" *I'd like that,* I almost said. Instead, I blurted out, "I'd better not."

Shutters slammed closed over the tentative light in his face. "Of course," he said. "I understand."

With a slight, polite nod, he turned and strode away, disappearing into the maw of a hangar.

Gee, couldn't I have said anything lamer, like *I have to wash my hair*? I cursed myself all the way back to my rooms.

*Idiot!* I told myself. *Why're you so upset? What're you ashamed of?*

Standing in the middle of my bedroom, I ragged on myself in this fashion, not paying attention to the gentle twilight outside the French doors, or Lucy hovering uncertainly in the doorway to the bathroom, or a familiar, sweetish, musky smell.

She drifted toward me, then back to the bathroom door. I ignored her. I had a few more choice words for myself. She came back and planted herself (if a ghost can plant itself) in front of me.

"*What*, Lucy?"

She beckoned. If she'd been alive, I would've said she was excited. She looked toward the bathroom.

"You want me to go in there?"

I felt like I was in a *Lassie* movie: *What, girl? Timmy is trapped in an old well?*

She nodded and beckoned again.

I sighed. "Okay. I need the distraction anyway."

The smell was stronger in the bathroom, but it still didn't register as anything unusual. I looked around. Same Roman tub, same brass tap, same tile and sink and toilet.

"I'm sorry," I said. "I don't see what you're all worked up about."

She took my hand—actually took my hand—with a cold, tingly and not entirely solid grip. She towed me to the tub and pointed down at the drain.

I dutifully looked. "Yep, I see the drain. What's so special—"

She took a tenuous finger and tapped my nose.

Finally, the smell registered. Mildew. Or mold. At first I still didn't put two and two together and suddenly, the lightbulb came on.

I fell to my knees beside the tub. Reaching down, I stuck a finger in the brushed brass drain and felt around inside it. It was slimy. I pulled out my finger and squinted at the grayish-blackish residue on it.

If I'd had any doubt before, my magic leapt up like a starved dog. I turned on the tap and hurriedly washed off the goop before it could grow into a hideous pulsating mass of hyphae.

Kneeling on the floor, I looked up at Lucy. "How? I didn't create this. It's just plain, old, ordinary drain gunk."

She held her hands palm up.

Okay, I told myself, don't get excited. It's only mold. It hardly even counts as life. For all I know, it's been around all the time and only took a regularly-used drain to make it noticeable.

Yeah, I argued, but Cerberus had said nothing *can* live here.

But what did he know? He was just a figment of

Hadis' imagination. Besides, a moldy drain didn't do a thing for my problem, and it wasn't about to make my stay any more pleasant.

And I didn't want to keep thinking about what might.

# VI

It's a very, very bad sign when the captive starts looking forward to the captor's company.

I'd been in bed a while. Every time I started to drift off, that thought would stick me with a pin then skitter away. Finally I caught it. I sat up straight, suddenly wide awake, that realization slamming through me like adrenaline.

It was still "night" outside, utterly dark, silent, lifeless as no night ever is in the real world. I scrambled up, my pulse jumping everywhere in my body from toes to eyeballs, like my blood pressure had instantly soared by twenty points.

Hello, Earth to Perry—Hadis was the only one here to be *with*. But that was exactly the point. How far could I expect this to go?

I didn't want to stick around to find out.

Never mind that my success in finding an escape route had so far been nil. I dragged clothes out of the closet, hurried them on and spilled out of the room.

I was out in the black hall without remembering the doors and hallways in between. In the silence, my blood sucked and rushed in my ears like the pound of waves on a beach. And then I heard...*whistling*.

At this point, I was so wigged out I jumped and flattened myself against the nearest wall.

The door to Hadis' throne room opened, and a man walked out.

At the moment, I wasn't particularly anxious for another tête-à-tête with Hadis. This, however, was not Hadis—I could tell that even from all the way across the hall. This was someone else, someone with light-colored hair in a military buzz who didn't cut the figure Hadis did, someone who was bopping along like he'd just won the lottery. Whistling.

Who in the *hell* could be in a good enough mood here to do that?

Who else could be here at all?

He disappeared through the bearded-man door. I stood leaning against my wall for a few more minutes, trying to decide if I'd seen what I thought I had. Of course, there was only one way to find out. I hurried after him.

The white globes cast their moonlike light across the anteroom, enough that I could clearly make out the figure walking away from me. He got to the last of the lights and three more figures faded out of the dimness to meet him.

He stopped and said, "All right, girls. I got the master talked around. He knows he's got to take care of business. Can't have the whole damn place fall apart around our ears."

Sure enough, the three new ones were women. There was a white girl with long, inky-black hair, a black girl with long, glimmering white hair, and a girl of indeterminate mixed race with flaming red hair.

All three were bigger and taller than the guy, which wasn't saying much because from where I stood, he looked short and a little bandy-legged.

The black-haired one said, "No barbecue tonight, I guess."

"Don't you get started, girl," said the white-haired one. "You make the master mad now and there we'll be, behind Cerberus' door."

"He wouldn't do that," the red-haired one said. "He's always fair, and *we* didn't upset him —"

"Got the little princess here," the black-haired woman interrupted. "Did you know that?"

I wondered who "the little princess" was until all four turned and looked in my direction.

Oh.

"Well, come on then," the man said. "Let's have a look at you."

"Yeah," the redhead said. "See what all the fuss is about."

Gosh, nothing like a friendly invitation. But the alternative was to tuck tail and run, so I shot my cuffs and strode forward. After all, I *am* a sorceress, and have my dignity to uphold.

They watched me approach with everything from sullen hostility to curiosity and amusement, and I had a chance to check them out.

To begin with, they were beautiful in spite of their outlandish looks. And outlandish they definitely were. The black-haired one wore tight motorcycle leathers. The white-haired one wore a formal ball gown complete with pearls, high-heeled pumps and elbow-length gloves. The red-haired one wore an interesting collection of cashmere sweater, chenille scarf sewn with small, round mirrors, green-and-pink-striped leggings and high-top sneakers.

The man, on the other hand, looked like a cross between George Burns and Popeye the Sailor, a grinning imp with a wrestler's arms and shoulders.

All four looked me up and down, then the man whistled again and said, "Not bad."

"Yeah, well, babes are a dime a dozen," the black-haired woman said. "If that's what the master wants, we could bring some that'd be less trouble."

"I'm Perry." I said firmly. "And you are?"

"Ah, now see, girls?" the man said. "We're being rude and here she is, the master's special guest." He gestured to the black girl with the white hair. "This beautiful young lady is Tissy."

"I'm Alex," the black-haired one broke in, "and that's Meg."

The redhead nodded and gave a crooked smile.

The man put a hand on his chest. "Me, I'm Ron Char. You can call me Ron."

He had a funny Eastern-sounding accent that flattened out all the vowels, so it sounded like, *Ah'm Ron Chaah.*

"She can call me gone," Alex said. "I got work to do." She stalked off.

"We better go after her," Tissy said. "You know how she gets."

They turned to follow her. Taking my arm, Meg pulled me along. "Don't mind Alex. She's just upset because she didn't get her dinner. We usually eat after work."

"What do you do?" I asked.

Five pairs of feet should've made a lot of noise walking across that stony ground. Mine were the only ones that did.

"We're in charge of operations here, we are," Ron said. "See, the girls're in acquisitions, and me, I'm in shipping."

He chuckled as if at a joke. Tissy rolled her eyes and Meg shook her head, smiling.

"We bring in the goods," Meg explained. "It's a real satisfying job, but it can be hard work."

Was that was where the eggs and English muffins and dried flowers and so forth came from? I'd assumed Hadis conjured them.

"That's why Alex takes her barbecue so serious." Tissy flipped her white hair over one shoulder, and it shimmered like a waterfall. "And she figures you're the reason she didn't get it."

I felt like I'd dropped into a punk version of *Alice in Wonderland*. "Me! How's that?"

Ron gave my shoulder a rough pat. "Well, see now, the master's just not been hisself lately. A'course, he's not apt to say why, but we've all noticed it's been since a certain young lady come along. He's distracted. Tonight, he just sat on his throne with his chin in 'is hand and said, 'This ain't the time, Ron. I got other concerns.'"

Meg shot him a startled glance. "You told him how we found that one, didn't you? We don't bring 'em here on a whim."

"A'course I did," Ron said. "But he just says, 'Who am I to dispense justice?'" Ron shook his head and tutted. "You ought to take mercy on him, missy," he said to me. "He's in a state, let me tell you."

Justice? What did that have to do with anything? But I latched onto the comment that Hadis was "in a state." This was curiously comforting and uncomfortable at the same time.

"Excuse me," I said. "I'm the one kidnapped here. I'm sorry if Hadis is upset because of me, but frankly, the feeling is mutual."

The other three exchanged glances. "That's not like him," Meg said.

"What isn't?" I said.

Meg frowned. "Kidnapping innocents." She shook her head, her red hair blazing around her. "He's just not that type."

"That's a relief, I guess," I said. "But here I am."

Ron stuck his hand in his pocket, pulled out a coin and flipped it: *ping*. It winked golden in the dim air, the size of a silver dollar. "See, otherwise, I'd expect you to be carrying my coin. Then I'd row you on across."

Tissy grinned, showing teeth that would've looked at home in a jaguar's mouth. "And we escort only the most deserving."

I looked back and forth between them. "Escort? Are you talking about people?"

"Fuel," Tissy said firmly. "To keep the engine running around here."

Meg nodded, her face hard.

I had the feeling their gas stops definitely took place at morgues, not slaughterhouses. I probably should've been queasy picturing the dead, um... meat arriving along with the grocery bags, but I was getting more and more excited. If this bunch was bringing in people—okay, bodies—that meant there was a way out.

I looked expectantly around at the bleak, barren nowhere-ness of rock and lowering sky. The glassy dark flow of the River of Woe drew a sharp line through all the tumbled grey. Ahead, Alex stopped by what I thought was a big, black rock. She bent and shoved the rock into the water—where it floated. Oh. A boat.

*A boat.* The ringing excitement inside me turned into a jangling I was surprised wasn't audible.

"Come on, hurry, up," Alex called. "I'm hungry, and we're obviously not gonna get anything here."

"Are you going to the real world?" I asked, trying to sound casual.

"Where else?" Meg said and smiled. "See you 'round, Perry."

Alex hopped into the boat, not rocking it a bit. "Yak, yak. Let's go."

Tissy and Meg climbed in, three big women in

one small boat. It floated high as it had when empty. Ron turned to climb in, too.

I followed right behind. "Take me."

They all looked at me like I was crazy. Maybe I was for wanting to go with such an alarming group.

"Please," I said. "I can't stay here. It's not doing Hadis or me any good, can't you see that?"

Alex made a rude noise. "It's more than our skins're worth to take you anywhere, princess."

Behind her, Tissy made a face and mimed smacking her in the head.

Patting Alex's arm, Meg said to me, "Give it a chance. Maybe you'll find you do have something good."

I scrambled to the edge of the water. "Wait— please. At least take a message. Tell my mother I'm all right!"

Shaking his head, Ron got in, picked up a long pole from the bottom of the boat and shoved off the bank. "You got to talk to the master about that. Now don't go doing anything stupid, missy, like trying to swim after us. If ya don't drown yourself, you'll only end up with a bad cold."

The river purled past, swift and almost silent. "But—"

Shaking the pole at me, Ron said, "No buts. Now stay there. I'll be right back."

I waited until the boat was a dim blur on the water before I waded out. The water bit at my feet, my ankles like misery, bitter and chill. Despair enveloped me, utter, drowning hopelessness: I'd be here forever in this dim, dead, dreary world, never to see Mom's face again. I should just give up...

I scrambled back up the bank and the feeling faded. This was obviously called the River of Woe for a good reason.

I looked down into the water. Little dark threads furred some of the stones closest to the bank. Squatting down, I peered at them, wanting to pick one out of the water to see what it was. No way was I going to plunge my hand and arm into that water again, though.

I was looking around for a stick (silly me) to fish out one of those rocks when Ron's whistling echoed across the water again.

"Your feet're wet," he said when he dragged the boat out of the water. "At least you got sense enough to go no further than that."

"You could take me across," I shot back. "You know I'll try if you don't."

He grinned. "Probably, but I might as well tell you, this boat'll sink right under you unless I'm in it." He gave me an appraising glance. "Besides, you don't want to be over there all by your lonesome." He turned and started back the way we'd come.

I hurried after him. "Why? What's there?"

"Nothing you want run into. Hell, sugar, the *master* wants nothin' to do with that sort." He shrugged. "But what choice has he got? He is what he is. Nothin' can change that."

He was walking fast enough to keep a little ahead. Trying to change the subject, I decided. Well, sorry. It wasn't going to happen.

"So what about Meg and Tissy and Alex? What about you? Seems to me if whatever's on the other side of the river is so awful, you'd go another way."

"Still trying to find that loophole, eh?" He fell into step with me. "You ain't gonna find one there, 'cause we ain't the kind that can be bothered by suchlike. Me, I'm the boatman. And the girls are spooks, see? You ever hear that saying, Hell's got no fury like a spurned woman? Spurned women was what they was before they become spooks. Extremely angry spooks. Then the master come along and told 'em if they was going to go tormenting, they ought to at least torment them what deserve it. And me..." He flipped the coin again, *ping*. "My boat don't go nowhere lest I get my coin."

Eyeing him, I frowned. He was telling me stuff while managing to tell me not much of anything. "And then what?"

He slid me a sidelong look. "If you don't know already, it's for the master to tell you."

I slid him a look of my own. "Maybe I should ask when he dispenses justice?"

Turning to face me, he propped his fists on his hips. "If I was you, I'd forget about all that." He made a disgusted noise. "When did pretty girls get so smart, anyway?"

# VII

I'm sure I don't need to say I tried Ron's boat despite his warnings. I got a good dunking in the River of Woe for my trouble. Promptly plunging into despair as well as cold, deep water, I decided I might as well just sink to the bottom and end it all.

Except someone had finked, because the river had been ensorcelled to spit me back up on the shore, where I lay sputtering and shivering and cursing. The boat popped back to the surface then bobbed there, the river's current chuckling against its boards.

Dripping Woe-water, I sneezed. By the time I got back to my rooms, I had a full-fledged miserable cold, miserable colds being part of the River of Woe's magic, I suppose.

Somebody finked about the cold, too.

Propped against two or three pillows, I lay there with a head that felt like a stuffed squash when knocking came at the door. Lucy turned to answer it.

"No!" I whispered. "I'm not here!"

She fluttered uncertainly by the bed.

"Tell him I went exploring. Tell him I got pneumonia and died!" I snarled. "It'd serve him right. This is all his fault!"

She fluttered a moment more, then winked out.

"Whatever." I turned over and dropped my

throbbing, ten-ton head into the pillows.

"Perry."

I flopped over. Hadis stood there, somehow managing to look both angry and concerned at the same time. Damn Lucy, letting him in.

I rolled over again with a grunt.

He laid his hand on my face. I started to jerk away, but the chill of his magic felt like a cool cloth on my hot head.

"You're feverish."

"Well, duh. I'm sick!"

He removed his hand and let out an exasperated sigh. "Of course you are! Ron told me he'd explained the consequences of trying to cross that river. It was incredibly foolish and entirely unworthy of you."

And you know what? I was actually ashamed.

"Huh," I said, the snappiest repartee I could manage at the moment. How was I to know Ron hadn't been just trying to put the scare into me?

Hadis sighed again. "I'll be back momentarily."

I turned over. "Don't bother." I'm not sure if he heard me.

Sometime later something scraped at my bedside table. I twitched, but managed to keep from jumping. Hadis himself, as usual, had entered in utter silence.

"Here," he said. "This may help."

I just grunted again and stayed curled on my side.

"Shall I help you sit up?"

No *way* was I going to let him do that. Rolling upright, I said, "Look—"

He turned, lifted a tray from the table and settled it across my lap. Grapefruit. Buttered toast. A steaming cup of tea. Oh, *please*.

"See if I put in enough honey. Go on."

I took a sip. I really couldn't taste it, but the honey coated my sore throat and the tang of lemon chipped at the brick wall in my head. "It's fine." I grumbled.

"Eat, too."

I sighed. It looked like I wouldn't get rid of him until I played the good patient. I dutifully munched toast until a sneezing and coughing fit hit me. He whisked the tray off my lap and a tissue into my hand, which I promptly buried my face in. It was soft and smooth and didn't rasp my poor nose: one of those tissues with lotion. My eyes streaming, I peered at him.

"That should be better," he said, settling the tissue box by my elbow. "I would do more, but—" He turned a hand palm up. "This is one sphere in which my powers won't oblige me."

It occurred to me what I must look like, red nose, puffy face, tangled hair and all. Probably the only person of my acquaintance who'd ever seen me look worse was Mom, and she was my *mother*, for the gods' sake. My hideousness didn't seem to bother him, though, because he just gazed on me with gentle concern.

I plucked at the covers, tempted to pull them over my head. *Come on, Perry. Who cares?* It wasn't like I wanted to look good for him. But I finger-combed at my hair, trying to make it look like I was just raking it back.

He stood still, hands opening and closing at his sides then abruptly turned away, toward my dresser. A moment later he turned back with something I couldn't quite see in his hand.

Sitting down on the edge of the bed, he leaned toward me, holding out my hairbrush. "Let me…"

I didn't know what to do. I didn't flinch, but I must've been eyeing the brush warily. He stopped, drew back. Fumbling a little, he reversed it, offering me the handle. I took it, and he gained his feet just as awkwardly.

"I thought you — to spare you having to get up — " He made a tight gesture of frustration. "Excuse me. I should let you rest."

He fled — yes, *fled*. Not that he ran from the room or anything, but he left in a serious hurry, and definitely without looking back.

I set the brush on the bedside table, turned over and hugged a pillow. Who cared? There was nobody to look good for.

෨෬

But I dragged myself out of bed the next morning to wash up. My skin had that funny prickly-tender feeling of fever and sickness, and I fell back into bed afterwards.

I lay on my side staring at the hairbrush still on my bedside table. When I was younger, Mom had brushed my hair to soothe me when I was sick or sad. My scalp tingled as I imagined the feeling of the brush stroking my hair. But in my imagination, the hand that held it was a man's, large and strong and gentle...

The door out in the sitting room opened. I snapped my eyes closed as if asleep, changed my mind and turned away from the door, changed it again and wriggled upright, hastily stuffing pillows behind me.

Hadis appeared in the bedroom doorway, smiling. "Good morning! I see you're already awake. Did you sleep well?"

Apparently he'd decided to be Brisk and Cheerful.

"Pretty well, thanks," I said.

"Here's breakfast." He lowered the tray into my lap.

This morning it was orange juice, hot cereal, jam and a little pitcher of milk or cream. "Thanks," I said again.

While I poured milk over my cereal, he pulled a chair to the bedside. The hairbrush tugged at me. I refused to look at it, something I wouldn't have to worry about if he'd just *leave*. I spooned a bite. He sat silently by me, not staring but disturbingly present. I took another dogged bite, swallowed.

"I think—" I began just as he said, "I thought—"

We both stopped. Waving for him to go on, I took a sip of orange juice. It was fresh-squeezed. I imagined him with his sleeves rolled up, wearing an apron and juicing oranges in a cavernous, antiseptic kitchen someplace. My heart gave a funny little skip.

"I thought, if you would like, I might read to you." He held up a thick book he must've conjured out of the air, because I hadn't seen it a moment ago.

*Read* to me? Well, I guess streaming or satellite TV wasn't exactly an option here. I stirred my cereal, making jam and milk spirals. I just wanted him to go away, right? I should be mad at him—hate him, even. Except—I couldn't. Don't ask me why, I just couldn't.

"I doubt I'll be very good company," I said to my breakfast.

"That isn't necessary. Simply be as comfortable as you can, and I'll take care of the rest."

I must be a lot sicker than I thought. That had to be why the proposition held such wistful appeal.

I stirred my cereal some more, which was turning into a purplish gruel. "Okay."

His eyes crinkled with the warmth of his smile. "Good. Then finish your breakfast."

He took the tray when I was done and poured fresh, hot tea. When I struggled to rearrange my pillows, he reached behind me to fix them—all quietly, without fuss. Those little things that make you cranky when you're sick seemed to disappear.

I didn't even notice it then, because believe me, if I had, *that* would've made me cranky. I just sighed and leaned back, holding tea just the right temperature in my lap. It stayed the right temperature, too, although I didn't notice that at the time, either.

He got comfortable in his chair, leaned back and opened the book.

It was a Sherlock Holmes story, the one where the butler figures out a riddle to uncover a treasure. I lay against my pillows and watched him.

That dark, intense gaze of his was bent on the book on his knee. His fingers walked down the page as he read, lifted gracefully to the top to turn to the next page.

I relaxed, my eyes half-closing. Hadis' voice alternately took on Sherlock's ponderous tones, Dr. Watson's more straightforward speech.

As crappy as I felt, it seemed comforting, natural for him to be there. After all, we were both in the same predicament, both stuck in this cold, dead plane, missing our families, both caught by forces beyond our control —

A jolt went through me like a sudden voice in a room I'd thought was empty. I opened my eyes wide.

What was I thinking? The force beyond *my* control was Hadis, the very same one sitting in that chair reading the last lines of the story. What was wrong with me?

Frowning, I squirmed in bed. "That's dumb," I said when he finished. "If the guy was so smart, he should've known better than to ask that girl for help." I snorted. "Like she'd want anything to do with him after he hurt her."

Hadis closed the book over a finger. "Perhaps in his desperation, he deceived himself."

"In his greed, you mean. His *selfishness*."

I wasn't really irritated, but I didn't like the weird sympathy I felt. It was wrong. It was flat creepy.

"Yes, he was selfish. And fickle, which is unpardonable."

"I can think of a few things more unpardonable," I sniped back.

With a rueful smile, he stood. "You're tired. I should let you rest. Shall I bring you anything?"

What did it take to start a fight with him? Why did he have to be so damned patient? Maybe he knew what I doing. Or maybe he felt guilty. Or maybe—

Maybe I spent way too much time thinking about what he thought.

I folded my arms and turned away. "No," I said. "I don't want anything."

He tucked the book under his arm and walked to the door.

My conscience felt like a slug with salt sprinkled on it. "Hadis."

He turned.

"Thank you."

His lips tucked. "You're quite welcome, Perry. It's my pleasure."

After he left, I lay staring up at the ceiling. Something inside me whirled. What was I feeling? Okay, besides sick. Maybe I was just getting really lonely. Except loneliness should feel desperate and empty, while I felt...cared for. Protected.

*Excuse* me? This was my kidnapper!

And that was the Big Problem between us, wasn't it? My mode of arrival. My enforced stay.

Because of Aros' damned spell! I raked my hands through my hair.

What Hadis had done in bringing me—keeping me—wasn't even by choice. So then... The illusory sunlight splashed across the carpet seemed to fade. So did that mean his attentiveness was all part of his bewitchment?

Lucy drifted in and sat sympathetically on the edge of the bed. It didn't dip under her. I reached out my hand, and hers curled around it with a prickle of static electricity.

"Oh, Lucy," I whispered. "What am I going to do?"

༺༻

As I lay listening for the click of the door, I felt like a cliff diver perched on the precipitous edge. Fever, I told myself sternly. That was all that was behind this lightheaded flutter. After all, it wasn't like there was any novelty to Hadis' visits. He was quite the devoted nurse for someone who used dead bodies for his magic.

When I heard the door, I put my hands under the covers and locked my fingers together.

Hadis came into the room. Today he was dressed in a grey shirt with the slightest hint of green, the cuffs rolled to his forearms, a more colorful and more casual style than usual. Even his black hair swept comfortably across his forehead, not ruthlessly combed into order.

He studied me from the doorway. "You look better." Coming to the bedside, he leaned down, laid his hand on my forehead, my cheek. "You don't seem feverish any longer."

I looked up at him, and his fingers lingered on my cheek. Something in his gaze changed—I felt it, an almost physical touch. His magic shivered over me, prickling cold over my skin before molding me with warmth. An answering warmth rushed through me. Under the covers, my own fingers loosened and I stirred. Then his hand fell away.

An involuntary sound escaped me. I coughed to cover it. (Or maybe I just coughed because I still had a cold. Sure, about like that heat that went through me a second ago was fever.)

He turned away, ostensibly to pull up a chair.

I was *not* disappointed. "No book today?"

Okay, maybe I was afraid we weren't going to have our daily chapter. That was adequate cause for disappointment, right?

"If you're feeling up to it, we could play a game instead." He was back to Brisk and Cheerful.

I don't know why that made me feel even worse.

"A game," I repeated, imagining something clinical and weighty, like chess.

He set a box on top of the covers: Monopoly. A

little smile quirked the corners of his mouth. "Go ahead and set up the board."

What was with the smile? Rearranging myself to make a flat place on the bed, I lifted off the top of the box and unfolded the board, gathering up money, cards, dice. But instead of the usual players' pieces — the car, the hat, Scotty dog, battleship and so forth, there were only tiny, painted die-cast cars.

I raised my brows.

"Choose yours," he said, still with that enigmatic smile.

I shrugged, picked an orange one and rolled the dice.

All of a sudden, I sat behind the wheel of a car driving along the cracked pavement and weedy lots of a downscale neighborhood. A street sign beside me announced, "Baltic Avenue." It was purple. I squeaked and let go of the wheel, and was back in my bedroom.

"Sorceropoly," he said, grinning as broadly as the eighteen-year-old versions of himself I'd seen in the memory rooms.

"Sorcer—" I spluttered, then laughter bubbled up.

"You like it," he said.

Still chuckling, I nodded. "I do. What happens when I buy a house?"

He rolled the dice. "You'll have to find out."

I bought up Virginia, States Avenue and St. Charles Place and put my money down for a house as soon as I could.

Standing on the sidewalk beside trees only a little taller than I am, two-by-fours zipped up like a fall of dominoes in reverse, clapboards laddered up the walls, shingles scaled the roof. Before I knew it, the trees shaded a neat, green lawn and curtains peeked around the edges of the windows.

Yes, Sorceropoly was definitely superior to the original version. A number of purchases later, Hadis stood on the curving drive of my hilltop trophy house on Pacific Avenue, not coincidentally overlooking the Pacific Ocean.

He raised his brows. "You'll bankrupt me, Perry."

"I'm a capitalist, not a philanthropist."

"Hmph. I didn't realize the two were mutually exclusive."

I grinned. "I'm a *greedy* capitalist. Don't you want to see what you're paying rent for?"

"By all means." His rueful tone was completely at odds with the sparkle of enjoyment in his eyes.

My cheeks went warm and I ducked my head, but I felt the same pleasure showing him the magnificent view of the ocean out the picture windows, the kitchen with its granite countertops, the private deck off the master suite.

We leaned side-by-side on the redwood railing, looking down cliffs to the water spinning white lace around the rocks. A gull swept silently overhead.

Our elbows just touched. I tucked mine closer to my body and shifted over, comfortable, content to be by him. The salt wind teased our hair, and sunlight hammered a path of pure gold to the horizon…

Except that there was no sunlight, no breeze, no horizon. It was all illusion, every bit of it.

I closed my eyes, shutting out the view. No, not everything was illusion. Hadis was still there. And I still felt—

I pushed away from the railing and went inside. I didn't look back, but I imagined him gazing after me, confused, uncertain. Tears pushed into my eyes.

"Perry? Are you—"

"Just—running out of steam," I said quickly, blinking hard.

I turned. He looked just like I'd imagined him. The tears tried to muscle their way in again, but I forced a smile. "It gives me a good excuse to take mercy on you. See, I might be a greedy capitalist, but not a ruthless one."

"Thank the gods for that. I'm finished if I land on one of your hotels." This time, his light tone was belied by a searching look.

I turned away again before he could discover more. The beautiful house shimmered back into my beautiful bedroom, Hadis in the chair beside the bed, the Monopoly board between us.

We both gathered up money and deeds, a task that seemed inordinately engrossing. Too soon, the lid was back on the box.

He stood and put on a smile. "I hope you'll give me a chance to even the score."

I hated that smile crafted for my benefit. I hated

this pretending that everything was all right, the thought of him leaving with that worry and uncertainty.

I hated him leaving, period. I was tired of thinking about all the rest of it—where I was, how I'd gotten here, what was going to happen.

"Aren't you going to read?" I asked, then realized how petulant and demanding it sounded. "I mean, if you feel like it. If you don't have anything else to do. Maybe after lunch?"

He bowed his head. When it came up again, the fake smile had vanished. "What would you like to eat? Are you up to more demanding fare than chicken noodle soup?"

"Let's live dangerously. How about French onion?"

# VIII

L et me say only that I may wipe out Hadis in Monopoly every time, but he plays a mean game of Scrabble.

This state of affairs continued through several waxings and wanings of the "moon." My own cycle corresponded, so I guess the illusion must've reflected actual chronological time. And weeds were growing in the illusory meadow outside my bedroom. I wasn't quite sure why Hadis would add weeds to that beautiful meadow. More verisimilitude, I guess.

But strangely, I was beginning to get used to the place. I didn't feel so...cut off any more, so deprived and desperate.

You're probably asking, "What about Mom?" Believe me, so was I.

Every day. I'd promise myself *today* I'd have a serious talk with Hadis about it. Then I'd see him for the first time that day and watch his face, grim and dark, glow with that smile like a lantern gleaming to life. And I'd think: Mom will never forgive him for what he did, spell or no spell. I'll end up having to choose which one to hurt. Or, vaguely: I can't trust Zeusse to stay out of my business and not mess everything up.

And the quietest, most frightening whisper of all:

Aros will take off the spell, and then what?

These kinds of thoughts must've been what led to the dream.

In it, I was sitting in one of several rows of chairs in a room. Mom and Eleanor sat on one side of me, Zeusse and Aros on the other. I wondered what we were doing there, then I gradually noticed that Mom was dressed all in black. That was weird. Mom never dressed in black. So were Eleanor and Zeusse and Aros. A big, wooden planter sat on a table in front of us, and it held a Night's Crown unfurling leaves and brilliant white flowers as we watched.

Mom was crying—sobbing. "It's dead," she kept saying over and over. "How can it be dead?"

Her grief wrung me. I was afraid I'd start crying myself. I put my arms around her and held her, stroked her hair, kissed her wet cheek.

"No, Mom, look at it. It's alive—it's growing. Can't you see? Look how beautiful it is!"

You know how in dreams things change from one into another? Well, when I looked up again, the Night's Crown in the wooden planter had changed into a coffin, and Mom wasn't saying, "It's dead," she was saying, "*She's* dead."

"She should've listened to me," Zeusse said. "If she'd gotten married, none of this would've happened."

Aros threw an arm over the back of his chair. "Serves her right, after what she did to me."

Eleanor wasn't crying, but her face was white and

blank.

"It's all my fault. I didn't catch her. It's all my fault." She rocked in time to the words, as if to a song.

I reached across Mom to grab Eleanor's hand. "No, listen, I'm fine, really! I'm happy with Hadis. We got off to a bad start, but everything's okay now that I understand."

Believe it or not, this made perfect sense in the dream.

Mom stood up as if I wasn't there, as if she couldn't feel my arms around her, and approached the coffin. "Goodbye, baby. I'll never stop missing you."

"But Mom, I'm here!" I stood too.

Standing, I could see into the coffin. I could see myself, in the coffin. Like they always say at funerals, I looked peaceful.

Mom had a coin in her hand, a gold coin the size of a silver dollar. She lifted the dead hand of the me in the coffin, kissed the fingers and tucked the coin into them. "There, baby. That'll get you where you need to go."

I stared in horror. Ron, Meg, Tissy and Alex suddenly stood in a line on the other side of the casket. I wanted to take the coin out of my dead hand, but then I'd still be holding it.

I looked up at them. "She doesn't know what it means."

All three women grinned, showing their jaguar teeth. "Dinner tonight," Alex said, licking her lips.

Her tongue was long and pink, like an animal's.

"It's a mistake," I pleaded. "I haven't done anything to deserve it!"

Ron shook his head. "You got the coin. It says you do."

Beside me, Mom was sobbing so hard I thought she'd collapse.

"Oh gods, Mom. Please don't cry." Finally crying myself, I reached for her, but she wasn't there.

And then I woke up. My eyes were dry, but I gulped down sobs. How long had I been here? Months. And Mom, oh, Mom —

I scrambled out of bed. My hands shook as I got dressed, just putting on the first things I grabbed out of the closet.

I'd never tried hard enough to get out of here. If nothing else, I could've gone on that hunger strike. Hadis couldn't just let me starve to death. After all, what would be the point?

I ran out of my room and along the hallway, burst through the door into the black hall. The magic there pulsed and surged as I'd never felt it before. Lucy drifted toward me from somewhere.

"Where's Hadis?" I asked her.

She hestitated, fluttering, then moved toward the door I'd just come through. Cursing, I strode out into the hall. Even with the ring, the magic shoved at me, pushing me back. That was answer enough. Leaning forward, I struggled against the current that coursed away from the throne room door.

Yeah, I know. It was like in a cheap thriller, where the heroine knows there's a killer on the loose but when she hears something in the basement, she creeps down there anyway. Duh. Even when Lucy put herself in front of me, I kept going. Because I wasn't really thinking about all this resistance as any kind of warning, but rather as another ploy to keep me here, while my mother was surely going crazy with grief at home.

I flung open the doors. I hadn't been in Hadis' throne room since the first time. It looked now exactly as it had then, writhing fires, obsidian throne, cloaked and helmeted Dark Lord and all.

A couple of unidentifiable heaps lay on the floor at the bottom of the dais steps, but the figure standing beside them was definitely Ron. Those shoulders and arms couldn't belong to anyone else. Cerberus, sitting on his haunches by the door, swung all three heads around when I entered.

"Perry!" they all said at once. "You shouldn't be here."

"Sorry," I said, striding forward. "It's important."

The leaping fires whispered unintelligible words in my ears as I walked between them. I ignored them. Ron turned toward me, dismay on his face.

On the throne, Hadis towered to his feet. "Leave here, Perry." His voice boomed ominously in his helmet. "Now."

Any other time, I might've been intimidated or outraged by the tone of command. "Hadis, we've got to talk. Now."

I still couldn't quite figure out what the heaps on the floor were. One looked like a scarecrow, clothes on a frame of crumpled sticks. The other was more of a pile. Then the pile moved and a man's face peered out of it.

I stopped, startled, confused. The pile rose and transformed into a man, a man I'd never seen before.

Like some kind of dangerous animal, he went from a crouch to hurtling toward me all in one motion. Metal glinted in his hand.

Ron moved, those wrestler's arms reaching. The sound of three dogs snarling came from behind me, the scrabble of nails on stone.

I think I moved. I'm sure I must've—I couldn't have frozen like a stupid rabbit while that man lunged for me, while Ron lunged for him.

Hadis took a few steps down, his gauntleted hand outstretched, fingers crooked, grasping, and in an awful voice thundered, "*You will not touch her!*"

One second the guy was coming at me with a face full of cruelty and ugliness. Then he—he *withered* in front of me. The reaching hands and arms turned into bundles of sticks, the knife clattered to the floor. The face…

Oh, gods, the face. It was like watching a time-lapse recording of something dead and rotting. The skin crinkled up, brown and tight against the bone beneath. The lips pulled back in a rictus grin, eyeballs shriveled like raisins, the eyelids turned into translucent membranes, the nose collapsed into the hole underneath it.

The hideous stick fingers scraped down my neck, my front, and the—the *thing* struck me with a dry crunch and a puff of death smell.

I stumbled and fell, my mouth wide open and nothing coming out. Ron snatched the husk off me, and Hadis came down the dais steps in a rush and a swirl of black cloak. He lifted me, folded me against him, straining me close.

"Perry," he said. "Perry."

I was cold, so cold, shivering. I could still smell it, the stink of sweat and fear, the reek of something dead. My cold cheek was pressed against Hadis' chest. Magic surged and prickled, icy, powerful, yet warm and enveloping.

I stared at the sticks inside the clothes. Two piles, two scarecrows lying on the black floor, withered pumpkin faces gaping at me, the one who had just died, the one that had been dead already. A gold coin glinted on the floor between them.

Still shaking, I pushed away, away from the things on the floor, away from Hadis.

"Perry," he said again, reaching for me. "I have no choice—"

I staggered backward, out of his reach. My mouth worked, but nothing came out.

*Lord of Death Lord of Death* hiccupped through my mind like a skipping CD. He powers his magic with death, someone had told me. Death. They don't stay alive long. Nothing lives here. Nothing *can* live here. Nothing. But. Him.

I whirled and bolted down the causeway. Cerberus stood between me and the door, a three-headed monster. I ran toward him, though, rather than stop or turn. He scrambled out of my way and I was through the doors.

There in the black hall, I faltered. The doors were all closed against me. Magic hammered at me. I spun, dizzy, gagging. My thoughts spun, too, beating like bees trapped in a jar.

A girl in a long, flowing dress appeared in front of me — no, not a girl. A ghost. Lucy. She put her cold, tingly hands on my cheeks and held me, held me looking into her faceless face until I stopped twitching and whimpering. Then she swept me up, steering me toward the door with the armored figure.

"No." I could get that much out coherently.

The door opened and I stumbled through, Lucy still guiding me.

Cerberus wasn't there. I looked around for him, bewildered, until I remembered he was in Hadis' throne room. At first I thought she would take me through the door to Hadis' memories.

Panting, I was about to plant my feet when she turned the other way, towing me toward the maze of doors and hallways and staircases, where I'd never been.

I went with her. I was still panicky enough to associate somewhere I'd never been with somewhere

Hadis wouldn't look for me. We climbed stairs, hurried along a curving, black-and-white tiled hallway and through a door.

Cerberus had told me this was the specters' place, and that they could frighten. Ron had said the master didn't want anything to do with them. If I'd been capable of putting two and two together at that point, I never would've let Lucy drag me in there.

The place was a waking nightmare.

Specters committed murder, over and over again, always for greed, for lust, for simple, naked cruelty. Killing with every kind of weapon or no weapon at all. Innocent people set up for something they had that another wanted, victims tortured and slaughtered for the sheer, sick joy of it.

I would have torn away from Lucy and run, but I didn't know the way, how to get out of this terrible place. Relentless, she dragged me on.

Finally, another door opened. I wanted to close my eyes, but the screams and pleas and sounds of carnage were worse that way. And so when we walked out onto someone's screened porch where a girl with long, dark-blond hair sat on a wicker settee, I was ready, if one can ever be ready for that kind of thing, for the rapist or greedy relative who would end her young life.

She wore a long dress. Something about her seemed awfully familiar, but I couldn't think where I'd seen her before.

I flinched when the door to the house opened,

spilling light onto the dim porch, but the girl looked up and smiled. "Took your time, didn't you?"

Hadis stepped through the door—Hadis as a young man near my age, maybe a year or two older.

"No," I said and backed toward the door.

Lucy blocked the way, holding out her hands in a pleading gesture. I thought of what lay outside the door and stopped.

Hadis balanced a couple of glasses and a plate with a big slice of red velvet cake and two forks. In spite of having his hands full, he nudged the door open with his elbow—the sort of inconvenience a sorcerer has no need to endure.

"Admit it," he said. "You can't live without me."

"You know I can't." The young woman patted the seat beside her. "C'mere."

He sat, handing her a glass and arranging the plate on his knee.

She gave a sly smile and put the glass on the little table beside her. "Thanks, that's sweet, but I know something sweeter."

She took the cake from him and put it on the table, too. Sliding an arm around his neck, she pulled him to her and they started kissing.

I turned away. "I don't want to see this. Take me back—get me out of here."

Lucy shook her head, took my arms and turned me back. It was like the scenes outside—watch or listen. Either way, I couldn't escape.

It was pretty clear they'd been an item for some

time, because there was no shyness or first-time eagerness between them.

It wasn't so much now that I didn't want anywhere near Hadis, not even his memories, but that I felt like a voyeur. It was like the problems my magic caused all over again.

I turned away again. "No, Lucy. I'm telling you, I don't want to watch—"

Wait, I thought. This was the old Hadis, the one who smiled and laughed. One who, apparently, still didn't have any magic. *And he's older than me.* How could that be?

All of a sudden, there was silence. Then Hadis said, "Lucy?"

I spun. He wasn't looking up at my Lucy, the shade standing beside me, he was speaking to the woman in his arms.

"Lucy, what's wrong?"

Light glimmered on her arm where it hung down, slack. The shadow of his hand groped across the wall above him, then the porch light flicked on.

But his hand was still a good six inches from the switch.

Wait—could I be seeing the moment his powers first manifested?

He wasn't looking at anything but the woman. Her head had rolled to the side, and her hair curtained her face. Lucy—his Lucy, my Lucy.

I snapped around to stare at the glimmering shade beside me. My stomach felt like it shrank and disappeared with a small pop, then Hadis spoke again.

"Come on, Lucy, quit fooling around." He lifted her, but she lolled slack as a rag doll. A doll with the stuffing coming out. "Lucy?" His voice went up in the beginnings of terror. She wilted like a broken flower in a freezing wind. Hadis staggered away. "Lucy, oh gods, Lucy!"

A light blinked on in the house, then another. Footsteps ran across the floor.

"Hadis!" a woman's voice said. The door burst open, and his mother ran out, wearing only her nightgown. "What's wrong?"

Hunched over Lucy, Hadis made a harsh, sobbing sound. "Mother, you've got to help her, I don't know what happened!"

She hurried across the porch. "Let me see. Come, Hadis."

She put out her hand. Still making those awful, wracking sobs, he grabbed it. *And she collapsed.*

It happened faster this time, the withering, the flattening.

"Mother!" he screamed, scrabbling backward across the porch. He ran into a chair, and it toppled with a squeak of wicker.

More footsteps, then his father spilled out.

"No!" I shouted, leaping at him.

It happened again, it had already happened years ago — there was no stopping it. The two faces, so alike, mirrored horror, then Hadis' father fell to his knees beside the withered husk of his wife.

"Fix her, Dad," Hadis sobbed, childlike, crawling toward him. "Put her back the way she was!"

He didn't even touch his father—the violence of his emotions made it unnecessary. And his father joined his mother, a bundle of brown sticks in boxer shorts—three scarecrows lying on the porch.

Hadis screamed. And screamed, and screamed—

Sobbing, sobbing as hard and harshly as Hadis had been, I jammed my hands over my ears and ran into the house. The screams stopped abruptly as I stumbled into another memory, but the nightmare didn't.

Death, death, death, over and over. His brother and sisters first, though he screamed at them to keep away, get away, no, no. His big, ugly dog, old and arthritic now, the fish, the finches, every creature he loved. Neighbors. Friends. Ambulance drivers. Police officers. Birds dropped out of trees that blackened and withered.

I blundered sobbing through it, as unable to escape as Hadis. Then Lucy was there, holding my hand, drawing me through the nightmares, the kind you can never wake up from because they're real. The specters' casual murders afterwards were nothing now, just the gratuitous gore of movies.

Finally, finally, the door that opened showed the black-and-white tiled foyer. Cerberus paced there now. All three heads jerked around when I staggered through that door. I was sobbing so hard I could scarcely stand.

"Perry!" he said. "Are you well? We've been searching everywhere for you!"

I ran to him, flung my arms around one of his necks. "Oh, Cerberus. His magic is as bad as mine— no, worse. Everything *dies!* How can he stand it?"

The other two heads came down to snuffle me. "Who, my dear? What has made you cry so?"

"Hadis!" I gulped down sobs and let go. Wiping my face, I took a few steps toward the door. "Where is he?"

The three heads lowered and the lips stretched back. "That's why I was seeking you—"

"Is he where I left him?" I broke in. I had a bad feeling about this. A very, very bad feeling.

"Yes, but—"

I darted for the door before he could finish.

The black hall was bereft of magic, as still as the moment before the bullet slams home.

"Oh, gods," I muttered. If Hadis had finally gotten desperate enough to— because of me— No. Not now. Not when I finally understood—

I ran for the throne room doors, yanked them open and flung myself through.

Hadis, at the far end of the room on his throne, stood up. He still wore the Dark Lord outfit, but the helmet was gone.

I, on the other hand, almost collapsed with relief to see him whole and well.

"Hadis, I'm so sorry, I didn't know—" I stopped,

because someone stepped out of the glare of the fires. For a second I thought it was Ron, but this person was too tall and slim. It couldn't be— "*Aros?*"

Holding out his hands, he walked toward me. "Perry, are you all right? I didn't know what I'd find."

I was almost as disoriented as when Hadis had first brought me here: one shock after another. "What are you doing here?"

Aros took my hands and squeezed them, real, living flesh, with a living heart pushing warm blood through the veins. Here. How?

"Come on, Perry," he said. "I'm taking you home."

"Home?" I should've been happy. I *was* happy, but my happiness had a bump on the head and felt a little queasy.

Then Hadis said, "That's still under negotiation."

"What?" I said profoundly.

Hadis sat down and leaned an elbow on the arm of this throne. "Seems you're far more valuable than I'd realized. Did you know you're worth as many women as I should wish?"

I looked back and forth between them. "What are you saying?"

Hadis smiled. It was not the same smile as when he'd watched his family at Yuletide.

"Aros proposes a trade. He tells me there are women by the score who would give...anything...to be with a man such as myself. Should I allow you to go with him, he'll most obligingly provide them."

I just stood there for a minute, choking on a chunk of disgust.

Aros clasped my hand tighter. "Whatever it takes to bring her home."

Did he know? Did he have any idea what the results of such a bargain would be? How Hadis' magic worked, why Hadis was here, utterly alone, to begin with? Or was he just horse trading, like I was some prize mare?

Hadis' face was a mask of calm. I couldn't be sure, but I thought I saw a flicker of my own contempt.

"And?" I said.

"Well," he said. "*I* thought I'd leave it up to you, as you're the principal."

Now Aros was the one who looked dumbfounded.

A sense of satisfaction surged through me so powerful, it was all I could do not to grin. Aros' fingers tightened.

I yanked my hand free. "Why are you here, Aros?"

If possible, he looked even more befuddled than before. "I told you. To take—"

I gave a snort of disbelief. "Excuse me, but do you really believe I'll go anywhere with you after what you did?"

He put on a convincingly hurt and baffled face. "What did I do?"

"You're the one who put the damned spell on him

in the first place!" I stabbed a finger up at Hadis. "Are you trying to tell me you just now figured out where I was?"

"What spell?" he said quickly—a little too quickly. "He'd notice any magic I did on him."

"Exactly what I've pointed out a number of times," Hadis said from on high. "Nevertheless, she remains unconvinced."

I wrestled with a powerful desire to smack Aros. "Yeah, *sure* there's no spell." I said as pleasantly as I could manage. "Only the one you *pretended* to put on him after my—" I made little curly quotes with my fingers. "—*conquest* at the plant show. Gosh, what a miracle of deduction that you could ever find me. I'm impressed. Aren't you impressed, Hadis?"

"Tremendously," he replied.

Aros took me by the arms. "Perry, what's wrong with you? Has he brainwashed you?" He had the dashing hero down pat. All he needed was the cleft chin.

I shrugged out of his grasp. "You want to know what's wrong? I'll tell you. You've known where I was all along, because you might be a lot of things, Aros, but stupid isn't one of them. Zeusse knew about the spell, too, didn't he? He must have, since he quit harassing Mom and me after the plant show."

His blond brows came down. "I told him it wasn't necessary—" He broke off.

I gave a thin, hard smile. "Yes? Go on."

"Hadis seemed to have captured your interest,"

he said smoothly. "How was I to know you'd come here unwillingly?" He glanced at Hadis.

So did I, and saw what all those specters must've seen before he dispensed...justice. Then Aros' words caught me. I paused, running our conversation back through my head.

"Well, Aros," I said, "since you didn't think I was here against my will, why would I need rescuing?"

"You said— This place— I mean, it's obvious—" He spluttered to a stop.

"You've been negotiating with me as if Perry were my unwilling guest," Hadis said. "Which doesn't correspond with your current arguments."

Aros opened and shut his mouth.

I folded my arms. "Gotcha."

There was silence while Hadis and I stared at Aros, who looked like he'd forgotten his lines on opening night.

Finally, Hadis said, "How did you come here, Aros?" He spoke with the calmness of a judge.

The fires writhed up, hissing incomprehensible words.

It was impossible to tell if Aros was pale in that leaping, ruddy light, but sweat sparkled on his upper lip. "Gaia..."

"Ah," Hadis said. "She opened the way? And shielded you from my magic?"

"Yes." The voice of the fire almost ate Aros' single word.

"Yes," Hadis echoed. "And why should my own

grandmother help you?"

I should've been wondering the same thing, but all I could think was, *What? Gaia, his* grandmother?

Aros' eyes darted as if seeking escape. "She said because I— Since it's my—" Then he burst out, "It was only a joke! How was I to know what you'd do?"

"Finally!" I said. "You admit you put a spell on him!"

Power like a blast of icy air suddenly shivered off Hadis. "So," he said. "The shielding that allowed me to attend the plant show must have blunted my ability to sense your magic. I see."

It looked like he *did* see, too. Fury chased mortification chased appalled realization across his face, as if Aros' sort-of confession had undone the spell.

A poisonous vine suddenly seemed to twist around my windpipe, and I tore my gaze from what else I might see in Hadis' face.

White edges cracked around the edges of the fires, as if the flames themselves were freezing. He stood, took the dais steps slowly. His cloak slithered down behind him like a shadowy liquid.

"You've made me wrong Perry." Even with the softness of his voice, I could hear the same humiliation and fury.

He had a right to be mad, but I couldn't stand to see him ashamed. "You were wronged, too, Hadis."

Aros shot me a panicked, outraged glance.

Turning my comment aside with one black-gauntleted hand, Hadis continued, still addressing Aros, "You have reduced me to the level of those who find their way here to me. You've made me a thief and worse." His eyes narrowed as he took a step down, then another. "A criminal."

Oh, damn. I took a couple of steps that put me between them. "Excuse me," I said to Hadis, "but you were under duress. People under duress aren't responsible for what they do."

Much as I detested Aros, I did *not* want to see him end up a scarecrow at the bottom of the dais steps. And Hadis seemed angry enough for that to happen, whether he intended it or not.

Rounding on Aros, I demanded, "Why are you here? What do you expect to get out of it? Just go away!"

"This is your fault!" he blurted out. "You were so uptight! Any other girl would've—"

"Any other girl would've just melted when some jerk grabbed her like she was a nice, juicy hamburger and tried to take a bite out of her face?" I interrupted. "Please!"

Hadis surged down the last step. He and Aros were nearly the same height, but with all his black, the glint of metal on his clothing, the look of cold fury on his face, Hadis was far more menacing.

"You—" His hand shot out as if to seize Aros by the arm or shoulder, but I caught his forearm. He dropped his hand. The muscles of his jaw bunched. At last he said, "Get out of here, boy. What comes here, stays. Don't tempt me further to keep you, as well."

Aros stepped back, brushing imaginary dust from his clothes, but I saw how his hands shook. "Fine by me. I wanted to see how far Demetra would go, anyway. Zeusse and Gaia are the squeamish ones."

I felt like I'd tripped and fallen into icy water. "Wait a minute. What's going on with Mom?"

"Poor Demetra." Aros tsk-tsked, then said in a pouty voice, "She wants her baby back. Who would've thought she had it in her, the gentle earth sorceress puttering in the fields with the duds?" He shot a vindictive glance at Hadis. "She's been working hard—blights, drought, floods, storms. Hope you don't mind the competition."

At some point, Hadis had put his arm around me. Now his grip tightened. "*Get out*," he grated.

Aros' nasty look slid to me. "See, Perry? Things are working out just the way your honey likes them. He *likes* 'em dead."

Hadis released me and took a step, but Aros hurriedly backed up, turned his back on us both and stalked off down the causeway.

The doors closed behind him with a boom. The echo washed through me like ripples of sewage sludge.

Hadis turned to me. I couldn't look at him.

"I didn't even say to tell Mom I'm okay," I said, my voice quavering. "I didn't ask him to bring her."

"Perry—"

I held up a hand. "I'm really tired. If you'll excuse me, I think I'll just go lie down."

I wobbled off down the causeway. The fires didn't whisper in my ears this time, but my conscience more than made up for it.

People were dying because of me, if I could believe Aros' nasty little parting hints. But people would die if I'd agreed to a trade, too. And now that the spell was gone—

How long before Hadis' humiliation made him hate me? He'd been made into what he detested because of me, he'd been forced into emotions he didn't even own.

My stomach lurched over and my throat locked up again. Gods, it sounded like some kind of rape. It *was*, just not the physical kind.

All of a sudden, I was outside my door. I opened it, crossed to my bedroom and sank down on the bed.

Lucy came in and knelt beside it. I tried to whip up the desperation that had tortured me in those early days here, but I only felt...what? Tired. Exhausted, in fact, incapable of thinking, but that was all.

Someone—okay, yes, Hadis—knocked at the door, but I just lay there, staring at the ceiling.

Lucy got up and drifted that way. A minute later she came back in, Hadis behind her. He stood by the bed a moment, looking down at me, then sat. Neither of us spoke, and Lucy drifted off again. *Here it comes*, I thought.

"I'm sorry, Perry," he said.

That was definitely not what I expected. I hazarded a glance at him. "It's not your fault."

"It *is* my fault." He paused, long and painfully, then put a hand over his face. "It seemed so natural. So *reasonable* to bring you here."

I sat up. "Hadis, he admitted about the spell."

He dropped his hand. "The spell doesn't excuse it. Look what I've done to you! Exactly what *he* did, forcing himself on you."

"You have it backw—"

"When I think of that," he persisted, "I could—" He clenched a fist.

The chill crackle of magic, like a rush of cold air ahead of an avalanche, buffeted me. I took his fist in both my hands.

He looked down, loosed the fist and closed his fingers around mine. The ominous sense of gathering magic subsided. I just kept my mouth shut, afraid of where this subject might lead.

"No. I won't inflict upon you again what I do. What I—must do." He fell silent.

Stroking my hand as if soothing some distressed creature, he went on, "When my magic first came to me, I struck the earth with my fist, wishing only for it to swallow me. Instead, I found myself in this place. I have been here so long, you see, Perry, here where my powers can harm nothing. I created this palace, the rooms of my memory to visit sometimes. My sole source of companionship was a few shades, Ron Char and Cerberus, as well as the very worst I can find of cold-blooded murderers."

"But how…?" I ventured. "You came to the plant show."

"That was Gaia's doing, and it took all her great sorcery to make possible that short visit. And even so, I had to avoid coming too near any living thing." He shook his head. "I can't believe I allowed myself to be convinced to take part in such recklessness. Except that I was beyond desperation, and my grandmother had promised me a gift." He looked up. "The plant you made. And then you laughed and took my hand… Was it only Aros' magic that made me wish to hear your laugh again? That made me desire to keep your hand in mine? I can't believe any spell could give such pleasure, such joy, such hope."

I suddenly remembered that we'd met at the Night's Crown *before* Aros had cast his spell. Sunlight burst in my chest. He'd felt like that *before* the spell. Before!

"Maybe you've learned to control your power, Hadis," I said, like a little kid who thinks if you believe in something hard enough, it'll come true.

"I must still feed my magic, as magic must be fed," he said bitterly. "I told you I am the most powerful sorcerer you will ever see, but my magic is a ruthless master. The source of my power— You saw. You can't imagine what—what it was like—in the world of life."

I gripped his hand tighter. Bowing his head, he took my other hand, held both between his own. I wanted to smooth back his black hair, tell him I understood, I'd seen.

But how could I really know what it was like to kill everything I loved, to have to live in this dim, bleak place, without hope, always alone?

"I can no more help what I do than I can help breathing. I can only make it…" He turned his head, wincing away as if in pain. "…more palatable to my conscience. But what I learned today from Aros — that, I can help. That, I won't allow to continue." He raised his head. "I'm sending you home."

"Home?" I repeated. Oh, gods. Here it was, and I'd thought — it had seemed like —

His jaw worked as if he struggled to hold something back — or to speak.

"I love you, Perry," he finally said. "The spell may have convinced me to bring you here as I did, but it can have nothing to do with how I feel. It can't force me to keep you now, when my reason and feelings for you tell me otherwise."

Tears abruptly overflowed. Dammit! Why was I crying now?

"*If* Mom is really doing what Aros said," I said angrily. "*If* he's not just lying to get at me, all I have to do is tell her — show her — I'm okay. Then I can come back." At the set expression on his face, I said, "I *will*. You'll open the way for me, won't you?"

He gave a sad quirk of a smile. "You're an earth sorceress. You require life even as I require —" He stopped, then went on, "How could I be content knowing you're compelled into my company, as the only living thing here? It would be no different than the months I already compelled you to stay."

All this time I'd felt like a tropical orchid that had fallen off the back of a truck in the middle of the Mojave Desert. Now I shriveled at the thought of never seeing Hadis again. If only I could change his mind!

"What did you ask Gaia for?" I demanded. "The thing she wouldn't give you, when she gave you the Night's Crown instead?"

He squeezed my fingers and continued as if I hadn't spoken, "I can't allow you to stay here out of pity for me. I only hoped to make you think a little better of me...than I deserve, perhaps."

He hadn't answered me. But his non-answer gave me a pretty good idea of what he'd asked for—an end.

I started crying in earnest, although I managed not to sob. "It isn't pity!"

"It is when you have no joy in what you do," he said gently.

"But I—!"

He bent his head, kissed my fingers and loosed them. "Take what you wish—clothes, the Night's Crown. Anything."

He stood and pulled me to my feet. *I will have joy in staying with you!* I wanted to argue. But could I say it truthfully?

"I—" My voice broke. "I'll be right back," I

muttered, trailed into the bathroom and sat down on the edge of the tub. Somehow, I didn't feel quite as distressed in here. The drain mold, probably.

The way I look, I always had to suspect guys of only caring about...well, what's under my clothes. Aros being a perfect case in point. Hadis had proven—was proving at that moment—that he cared for *me*. How could I turn my back on that forever? I loved Mom, missed her, wanted to see Eleanor and my friends again, but they couldn't offer Hadis' devotion, his concern, his gentleness...his love.

I took a tissue and wiped my face. Could he be right? If I stayed here, would I be like those destitute young couples who swear their love is all that matters, only to discover that poverty tends to put a real damper on romance? I *did* need living and growing things around me. And Hadis *was* the only other living thing here. Well, the only living thing besides drain mold and the Night's Crown. Was that the only attraction to him—my magic asserting its need? That, and pity, as he said?

I dropped my head into my hands. I didn't know what I felt. I didn't know what I thought. Gods. How did everything get to be so complicated?

"Perry?" Hadis called from the bedroom. "Are you all right?"

The tissue in my fist was sodden. I grabbed another and wiped my face again. "I'm fine. Don't worry, just fine."

I didn't sound fine, though. My voice trembled

like…like I was crying.

Sure enough, he showed up in the doorway. Taking one grieved look at me, he said, "Perry—" Suddenly, he sniffed. "What is that smell?"

I sniffed, too, pretending I was only trying to identify what he smelled. "Oh," I quavered. "The drain."

His brows drew together a little. "What do you mean?"

After everything, here we were talking about the drain. "You know, slime growing in the drain. That's what's making the smell."

He gave me a single, sharp glance and strode out. Bewildered, I got up and followed.

The French doors sprang open ahead of him. Outside, the meadow had been turning grey with the coming "dawn."

In an instant it was fully light, the meadow gone. In its place was a dip and swell of rock and gravel under a blank, blazing white sky. But the landscape wasn't barren.

Greenery wandered in an uneven line from the porch down a gentle slope. It pooled in a rough circle about ten feet wide, the very spot, if I wasn't mistaken, where I'd sat and tried to open the way home my first day here. The growth wasn't anything beautiful or exciting like the Night's Crown, just common weeds—mallow, foxtail, burrclover, dandelion, the kinds of things that might've left seeds in the mud on a pair of dirty overalls.

Green. Growing. Alive. Here, in this place where nothing could live.

Hadis walked out onto the porch, his head slowly turning from side to side. I couldn't tell if he were shaking it in amazement or looking around the meadow. The air outside wafted in a scent of growing things.

I wobbled, so I put my hand on the back of a chair. No wonder I'd been feeling better lately.

"How—how did you do that? I thought—" I bit back reminding him what his magic did.

"I didn't do this." He shook his head and whispered in disbelief, "They aren't dying."

I trailed after him as my mind turned over, *tock, tock, tock*, like a pendulum clock approaching the hour. Then realization struck.

"*My* magic did this," I said in a small, astonished voice.

It wasn't just the oddity of the Night's Crown. It wasn't just the unlikelihood of my immunity. *It could make anything live and grow here.* Here, under the influence of magic as uncontrollably lethal as mine was uncontrollably fruitful.

I couldn't believe it any more than Hadis could.

He spun and caught me by the shoulders. "Do you have any idea what a miracle this is?" His face was alight with amazement, with joy.

"Do *you*?" I asked. "They aren't growing like crazy things. They're just..." I gestured, as amazed as he was. "...sitting there like rational plants."

I don't know if he heard me—he just gripped my shoulders and stared outside. Slow certainty began to sprout like a seed in me.

I raised my hand, touched his cheek, the curve of his smile. "Hadis."

He looked down at me, his face full of bewildered joy and disbelief.

"Do you know what this means?" I asked myself as much as him, because it meant my magic *couldn't* be compelling me toward him. "It means I can be with you."

Turning away, he leaned on the railing and gripped it hard. "Perry, don't."

My stomach did the same thing his hands were doing to the railing. "You don't want me here?"

He looked a little like a man on a desert island watching his rescue boat sink.

"Gods, it isn't that." He lifted one hand, made a wild gesture. "I can't let you bury yourself in this place!"

What was going on? Why was he upset?

"Hadis, I—"

"Don't you see, Perry? Your nature—and your wishes—won't allow you to stay month in and month out, year after year. And I—" He squeezed his eyes shut and clenched his jaw. Then he grated, "I can never go with you! I'll have to let you go, and when you choose to return, I'll have to let you go all over again, never knowing if next time you'll be able to bear to come back to me—"

He raised his head suddenly, looked past me. The furious anguish on his face subsided beneath a mask of imperfect calm. "Lucy? What is it?"

I turned quickly. Lucy hovered on the patch of weeds beyond the porch. My face went hot.

It was silly, really. After all, she was dead. Just a memory, Hadis had said. But she was my friend, and she'd loved him first.

She drifted shimmering across the green, following it like a path to us. As always, her face was turned away, but she took my hand. The stone in the ring Hadis had given me glittered like a raindrop when she pressed my hand to her cheek. She reached for Hadis' hand, pressed it to her other cheek.

"Oh, Lucy," I said.

Sorrow, confusion, hopeless love fluttered around in me like trapped sparrows. Hadis' face worked and his magic crackled in the air, nipping at the edges of leaves, prickling my skin.

And then Lucy started to glow.

At first I thought what she felt must be shining through her. But the glow became brighter, thinner, taller, arching upward and outward, torchlike. Our hands no longer rested on Lucy's cold, static-crackly cheek, but rather on each other. Hadis' magic, hot-cold like icy water, mixed with the familiar doglike exuberance of mine, twining into the brilliant green-white glow that was Lucy.

I didn't have a clue what was going on, but it didn't look like it was doing her any good. As a matter of fact, that glow completely engulfed her.

I tried to snatch my hand away. I was pretty sure Hadis wasn't holding it, but I couldn't pull free. And of course, my magic wasn't about to flick off the switch just because that's what I wanted.

Hadis, however, had a lot more years of wrestling with willful, recalcitrant magic than I did. Finally, he wrenched his hand out. Mine came with it, fingers tangled with his.

"Lucy!" I said, and—duh—reached for the glow again.

It was already fading, shrinking to a thin, white column. When my hand reached in, it touched smooth bark. Dancing leaves with white undersides rustled over my head, as if with whispery laughter.

Hadis ran tentative fingers along the trunk. "A tree," he said wonderingly.

"White poplar," I corrected automatically.

He looked a lot like I must've when he first brought me to his realm. "She's—she was—only a shade. All she did was a reflection of my wishes. She had nothing in her—no soul—how could she have done more?"

"Why?" I demanded. "Why did she make us turn her into a tree?"

The shadows of her leaves made lace where a patch of dandelions pushed through the gravel. A thought—a feeling as impossible and insubstantial as those leaf shadows—brushed through my mind.

I took his hand. "Come with me."

I stepped off the porch, pulling him with me. He hesitated, glancing past me at the straggling growth of weeds, but I kept tugging. Finally he stepped onto a patch of mallow.

I remembered those dead spots in the lawn like footprints so long ago. Urging him on, I watched the mallows. When he lifted his foot, the little round, crinkly leaves slowly sprang back upright. Yellow dandelion flowers brushed his boots. Burrclover nodded in the slight breeze of his movement.

"Touch them," I said.

As if hypnotized, he bent slowly and ran a brilliant green blade of foxtail through his fingers.

He straightened, reached up, traced the outline of a leaf—Lucy's leaf—with one finger. It flashed like wings, green and white.

"We did this," he said. "We. With our magic. Together. She wanted us—me—to understand."

And he laughed. He picked me up and swung me around, laughing.

It's not easy to think—much less talk—when you're being spun around in circles, but by the time he put me down, I'd managed to put two and two together.

"You don't have to stay here."

He smiled down at me like a floodlight at a grand opening. "Not while I'm with you."

I looked up into the branches of Lucy's tree. The leaves fluttered, dancing with life. With *life*. Looking at Hadis again, I saw the joyful, buoyant face I'd only seen in the rooms behind Cerberus' door. Pity was definitely not part of the picture here.

I held out my hands. The blue stone of the ring he'd given me sparkled in the flat, white light.

"Hadis." I pulled off the ring, slipped it onto my left hand. "Let's get married."

I tucked my fingers into the front of his shirt and pulled. His eyes went wide, but he didn't resist. Then I kissed him a little more suggestively than his mother had kissed his father the first time I'd seen them.

I don't know what it did to him, but as far as I was concerned, whoa!

He closed his eyes and took a long breath. Opening them again, he lifted his hands and ran his fingers through my hair. My knees nearly went out from under me right there.

Fortunately he picked me up and carried me to the bed.

&#8734;&#8451;&#8450;

If you've read the tabloid articles ("*Woman Abducted by Practitioner of Dark Magic — Omens of End Days Seen!*"), you're probably wondering where the pomegranate comes in. You know, the one I supposedly ate a few seeds from, thus forcing me to stay in Hadis' realm? Actually, it's just a pretty, poetic metaphor for what happened next—the bright jewels of seeds, the sweet juice…

Um, you get the idea. Anyway, I can promise you I didn't go ten months without *eating*.

Needless to say, Mom was overjoyed to see me. She was definitely not thrilled to see Hadis beside me, fingers entwined with mine, but she got over it once she got to know him, and once she saw how happy we are together.

Every year we spend from Thanksgiving until Easter with her, although we travel to places with four seasons, like New England or Colorado. That way if anyone's magic gets out of hand, it isn't too noticeable. But in general, we tend to balance each other out.

My garden is growing nicely on his plane. Gaia is supposed to come see it next spring, give me some tips on how to handle a new ecosystem, since cattails and tulies and young willows and blackberries are growing now by the River of Woe.

I keep telling Hadis we should change the name to the River of Whoa. After all, if I hadn't caught that miserable cold, we might not be enjoying those pomegranates now.

❧☙

Also by K. Lynn Bay:

**CHANCESHAPER**

*By K. Lynn Bay writing as* Kathlena L. Contreras:

**FAMILIAR MAGIC**

**SHADOWBOUND**

## ABOUT THE AUTHOR

In other incarnations, K. Lynn Bay has been a small business owner, an assistant medical librarian, a data manager, and a pusher of paper in countless offices. She currently lives with her husband, five dogs and assorted livestock on the edge of the woods above the valley east of Albuquerque, New Mexico, USA, a place where the view goes on forever.

K. Lynn Bay also writes as Kathlena L. Contreras.